Cassie didn't know what had come over her but being in Heath's embrace was amazing.

She was a little embarrassed by her behavior, but by the time she'd regained her wits and backed away, word came that the newborn was in the nursery. She dragged Heath out of the waiting room and rushed down the hall to the wide glass panes. She'd worry about the hug later.

A row of tiny swaddled babies lined the nursery. "Oh, my goodness." Cassie pressed closer to the pane, snapping photos with her cell phone. "He's beautiful. Look at him, Heath. He's wonderful. So tiny and tough and precious."

"Your brother is a blessed man."

"Blessed," Cassie murmured, thinking Heath used exactly the right word. With uncharacteristic neediness, she battled the urge to lean her head on the lawman's sturdy, dependable shoulder.

Something powerful turned over in her chest.

Books by Linda Goodnight

Love Inspired

In the Spirit of...Christmas
A Very Special Delivery
*A Season for Grace
*A Touch of Grace
*The Heart of Grace
Missionary Daddy
A Time to Heal
Home to Crossroads Ranch
The Baby Bond
†Finding Her Way Home
†The Wedding Garden
The Lawman's Christmas Wish
†A Place to Belong
The Nanny's Homecoming

†The Christmas Child
†The Last Bridge Home
A Snowglobe Christmas
    "Yuletide Homecoming"
**Rancher's Refuge
**Baby in His Arms
**Sugarplum Homecoming
**The Lawman's Honor

*The Brothers' Bond
†Redemption River
**Whisper Falls

LINDA GOODNIGHT

Winner of a RITA® Award for excellence in inspirational fiction, Linda Goodnight has also won a Booksellers' Best Award, an ACFW Book of the Year award and a Reviewers' Choice Award from *RT Book Reviews*. Linda has appeared on the Christian bestseller list and her romance novels have been translated into more than a dozen languages. Active in orphan ministry, this former nurse and teacher enjoys writing fiction that carries a message of hope and light in a sometimes dark world. She and her husband live in Oklahoma. Visit her website at www.lindagoodnight.com. To browse a current listing of Linda Goodnight's titles, please visit www.Harlequin.com.

The Lawman's Honor
Linda Goodnight

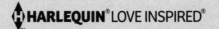

HARLEQUIN® LOVE INSPIRED®

The entire Whisper Falls series is dedicated
to the memory of my brother, Stan Case.

Recycling programs
for this product may
not exist in your area.

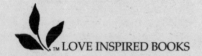

™ LOVE INSPIRED BOOKS

ISBN-13: 978-0-373-87871-0

THE LAWMAN'S HONOR

Copyright © 2014 by Linda Goodnight

www.Harlequin.com

Printed in U.S.A.

Immediately Jesus made His disciples get into the boat and go before Him to the other side, while He sent the multitudes away. And when He had sent the multitudes away, He went up on the mountain by Himself to pray. Now when evening came, He was alone there. But the boat was now in the middle of the sea, tossed by the waves, for the wind was contrary…. And they cried out for fear.
But immediately Jesus spoke to them, saying, "Be of good cheer! It is I; do not be afraid."
—*Matthew* 14:22–27

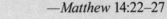

Rumor says that if a prayer is murmured beneath Whisper Falls, God will hear and answer. Some folks think it's superstitious nonsense. Some think it's a clever ploy to attract tourists. Others believe that God works in mysterious ways, and prayers, no matter where whispered, are always heard.

Prologue

She was probably crazy for doing this. As a local, she should know better. Climbing Whisper Falls to pray was a rumor, a myth, a publicity stunt. But for reasons she couldn't explain or deny, Cassie Blackwell felt the need to do it anyway. Her sister-in-law had prayed here and look how well that had turned out.

Sticking one boot against the wall of slippery rocks, Cassie started the ascent. Whisper Falls sprayed water against the side of her face as it tumbled to the pool below. Spring was here and with it the Blackberry River rushing wildly to embrace the sea like a long lost love.

Feeling self-conscious, Cassie glanced below—and promptly wished she hadn't. Her stomach rose into her throat, shortening her breath. The top was a long way from the bottom, the roar of the falls a deafening threat to safety.

With a firm admonishment not to look down again, she turned her gaze to the cliff top. No one else was here in the remote wooded area. Thank goodness. No one would ever know the ridiculous thing she'd done. Clinging now to the dampness, digging in with her fingers and toes, she clambered up and, with heart banging against her rib cage,

Cassie catapulted onto the narrow ledge behind the cascade of magnificent white foam.

The inner sanctum behind the falls was stunningly quiet. She took a minute to catch her breath and soak up the atmosphere. It was beautiful, peaceful and private as though the world below was another universe.

"Will Heaven be like this, Lord?" she asked, awed, for she knew in that moment what others before her had discovered. God was here. Oh, sure, she believed He was everywhere, but something about this place seemed spiritual.

So she lifted her face to the astounding sight above her and prayed.

"Father God, it's me, Cassie. Since the funeral, I've been numb, like I'm frozen inside. I don't know how to fix it. I don't know how to make the emptiness go away. I want to feel again."

There was a certain fear in admitting such a thing. It was as if she was throwing away what she and Darrell had shared. But she would never do that. And yet, she wanted something. No, she *needed* something. The problem? She didn't know what that something was. But with all her heart, she prayed that God would know and answer.

Chapter One

The rain had started a few miles back. On a moonless black night on an unfamiliar rural road, a man could easily get lost. Heath Monroe had a feeling he might have done exactly that.

He cast a cautious eye at the sky, at jagged streaks of lightning in approaching clouds. This section of the Ozarks was in for a storm. Hopefully, he could find the little town of Whisper Falls before the worst of it struck.

Heath was weary from the long drive, and his GPS had long ago stopped telling the truth. When he'd pulled off for gasoline at a tiny whistle-stop community no bigger than a convenience store and a handful of houses, he'd grabbed some junk food to hold him over. He'd eaten worse and certainly gone longer without healthy food. The friendly woman at the store assured him he was headed in the right direction.

"Keep going until you see the turnoff," she'd said. "It's kind of hard to see at night but there's a little green sign."

A muscle in his left shoulder had tightened and the pain now ran up the side of his neck. Heath exhaled through his lips, eager to find that road sign.

But it wasn't only the drive making him weary. He was

soul weary, the only reason he could think of for his sudden decision to exchange a job he'd loved for work in a small Ozark town. He was tired of the constant travel, the short-circuited relationships that were over before they had a chance, and worst of all, the feeling that he was trying to empty the ocean with a teaspoon.

And yet, he was driven to keep fighting. His father had taught him that. Never give up. Right the wrongs. Fight the fight. He was an army of one. One man could change the world.

Heath took a hand from the wheel to touch the badge in his pants pocket. His father's life mattered and Heath aimed to carry the torch. *Had* carried it for a lot of years. The new assignment was different but the overriding mission remained the same.

Thunder rumbled in the distance.

"Couldn't be too much farther." He'd give Mom and Holt a call as soon as he hit town. They'd both be worried, his brother as much as his mother. After all the places he'd been, the training he'd received and all his successful missions, Mom still feared he'd end up like his father.

He hoped she was wrong, but he couldn't count on it.

Cassie Blackwell hunched over the steering wheel and squinted through the rain-lashed windshield. Wind buffeted the dependable little Nissan as a clap of thunder vibrated through Cassie's bones. She shivered, though the heater pumped out plenty of clammy warmth. Her eyes burned from staring into the pitch-black night lit only by the pale wash of headlights and the frequent, unpredictable lightning.

In the last ten minutes, the storm had gotten progressively worse. Scary bad.

Like blue laser fingers, lightning suddenly splayed

across the ominous clouds. As if the skies had opened, rain fell in sheets, loud and unnerving. The lightning was quickly sucked back into the swirling masses overhead, into a blackness so deep Cassie couldn't tell for sure where she was.

This looked bad. Real bad. Tornado season was upon them and though she was no meteorologist, she understood tornadic thunderstorms. Texans cut their teeth on tornados, and a half dozen years in the Ozarks couldn't erase a life-time of experience.

Through the deluge, she spotted the car ahead. One lone vehicle other than hers crawled through the night, cling-ing to the curvy mountain roadway. It reminded Cassie of a commercial in which the tires had grown tiger claws to grip the pavement. Tonight her Nissan needed claws.

If a tornado fell out of those ominous clouds, she didn't know what she'd do. There was no ditch, no storm shel-ter, no houses for miles, other than her own still a dozen miles ahead.

Her eyes had started to burn from the strain of peering into the astonishing blackness. The air was sticky, a har-binger. Small hail ping-ponged off the hood and bounced in the headlights like popcorn on the blacktop. Her wind-shield wipers kept up a rhythmic *whap-whap* to battle the sluicing rain, a battle they couldn't win tonight.

She punched on the radio, hoping for weather reports. Static, intensified by sizzles of lightning, filled the car. She turned off the useless noise. Whatever the weather, she would have to ride it out.

Normally, Cassie loved thunderstorms. The clean smell, the invigorating wind, the sudden burst of cold wetness. Most of all she enjoyed the wild, showy side of nature, the power of an awesome God. She liked to sit on the ranch's front porch and watch the storms move over the mountains, to wrap in a blanket and sip a cup of hot tea and dream of the one and only time she and Darrell had gotten to do that very thing together. Before they married. Before he was gone.

Lightning flared in the sky for scant seconds. Cassie noticed the car again, its watery red taillights barely discernible through the deep black curtain of heavy rain. She watched the lights waver and then fishtail crazily as the driver lost control.

"Jesus!" Cassie cried, a prayer for the driver. The lightning disappeared as quickly as it had come. In the blackness, she didn't know if the car had righted itself or if even now, the driver plunged down an incline into the thick woods…or worse, into one of the canyons.

She dared not speed up, lest she, too, lose control. The road curved sharply ahead where she'd last seen the other vehicle. She crept forward, a prayer on her lips, her eyes wide and scratchy as she tried to make out the exact spot where she'd seen the driver lose control.

There. Cassie decelerated and tapped her brake. To her right and fifty feet down into a deep ravine she spotted the faint impression of light. Dread in her gut, heart racing, she pulled as far to the side of the road as possible and stopped. The rain still came in drenching torrents. Storm or not, she had to do something. Someone could be hurt.

Cell phones were great when they worked, which was rarely the case in remote areas like this one. In this storm she had serious doubts, but she quickly pressed 911 anyway. When nothing happened, she fired a text to her brother and another to Police Chief JoEtta Farnsworth in the nearest town, Whisper Falls. Maybe, just maybe, the text could get through the storm.

Then, she did what she had to do. Flashlight in hand, she

leaped out into the wild, raging night and plunged down the brushy incline toward the accident.

In seconds she was drenched. Brush grabbed at her naked legs, ripping flesh. Of all the crummy times to wear a skirt. Slipping and sliding, Cassie stumbled once on a fallen tree her light hadn't picked up. A bolt of lightning, blue with fire, had her up and scurrying faster. Old leaves mushy with rain squished beneath her pretty new heels, a gift from her mother from only yesterday.

Through the noisy storm, she heard the rumble of a motor. The vehicle, which she now saw was a smaller SUV, was still running, the headlights eerie in the deep, tangled woods.

Cassie ran to the driver's side and pounded on the window. "Hello. Are you all right? Hello!"

A dark form slumped over the steering wheel. Shaking now, from both cold and anxiety, Cassie pulled at the back door. Locked. Frustrated, she banged on the driver's window.

"Wake up. Wake up." She prayed he wasn't dead. The last dead person she'd seen had been her husband.

Darrell's lifeless face flashed in her mental viewer. She shook her head to dispel the image.

Shivering, face dripping rain, hair plastered against her skull and vision skewed by the torrent, she shined the flashlight toward the ground, searching for anything to break out a window. Finding a thick branch, she heaved it against the back passenger glass. Nothing other than a jarred wrist for her efforts.

She hurried to the front of the car. The windshield had spider-webbed in the crash but hadn't given way. It was weak. She could possibly break through the glass, much as she disliked the idea of exposing the injured driver to a flood of rain. She started around the car to the passenger's side. Better to break the windshield out on the side farthest from the driver.

Behind her, the driver's door popped. In a burst of adrenaline, Cassie whirled toward the sound. The dark woods were eerie and she was alone. Her flashlight picked out a man's hand and wrist on the armrest. A watch glowed green in the darkness right before the arm fell, limp.

Cassie hurried to the door and pulled, but the door had opened as far as it could. Only a few inches. Her fingers fumbled around inside the door and found the locks, popping them.

"Thank You, Lord."

She yanked the back door open and crawled inside, shivering at the interior warmth and the sudden, wonderful cessation of rain. Rain dripped all over the nice leather interior, but that was the least of her worries.

She shook the broad shoulder in front of her. "Can you hear me?"

He mumbled something.

Cassie shined the flashlight at the side of his face and scrambled over the seat, leaving a trail of water.

The man's face turned slightly toward her. "What—?"

"Where are you hurt?"

"Hurt?"

He must be addled, concussed or…something. She owned a beauty salon. What did she know about injuries other than sunburn from too much time in the tanning beds?

"Do you think you can walk? I have my car up on the road. I can take you to a doctor." Dr. Ron, the only physician in Whisper Falls, was accustomed to being awakened in the night for emergencies.

He shook his head. "My leg."

What about his leg? Was it broken? Crushed? Were

bones sticking out? The last, grizzly thought rattled her nerves but bones or not, she was his only help.

Using the flashlight, Cassie started at the top of his head and began a slow perusal of the driver. "I can't see that well, but let me check you over. I texted for help. I don't know if I had reception though. The storm."

He nodded, his jaw tight and lines of pain radiating from his lips all the way into the stretched cords of his neck. His was a manly face with wide, chiseled jawbones and deep-set eyes. She couldn't tell the color but she could see the pain and confusion. He was addled, no doubt about it.

She'd never been much for facial hair but his suited. A wisp of whiskers above his lip and on his chin. Just a little, just enough to make a woman notice. Not that she was noticing in a situation like this.

"Forgive the intrusion," she murmured, not sure if he heard or understood, but her vision was limited. His medium-length dark hair could easily conceal a wound. She had no choice but to touch him. "Are you bleeding anywhere?"

Her fingers scanned the back of his head, up and over to the forehead. There. A knot the size of a softball along his left temple. "You've hit your head."

She pulled her fingers back and shined the light on them. No blood. She breathed a sigh of relief. No blood suited her fine.

"My leg," he said again and attempted a slight shift in the seat.

Cassie aimed the light lower, searching in the dimness. "I can't see."

He reached above his head and snapped on the dome light. He wasn't as addled as she'd thought. *She* hadn't thought of that.

Cassie blinked against the brightness. "Thanks."

"What happened?"

Or maybe he was. "You missed the curve and hit a tree."

That was the short version.

"My leg. What happened?"

"I can't tell. I think it might be stuck. Can you move it at all?" Beneath the dash was a crumpled mess of metal and wires. She didn't want to think about his leg underneath that weight.

"No."

"Does it hurt?"

He paused as if having to think about the question. "I don't think so."

Strange answer. Either it did or it didn't.

She shined the light in his face. Glazed eyes barely blinked.

Okay, this was not good. The man had a head injury and couldn't get out of the car. And it was likely her text hadn't gone through.

Thunder rumbled. Rain kept up a steady swoosh. Flashes of lightning radiated through the night sky.

She did not want to make that trip back up to the road.

"Will you be all right while I go to my car and try to call again? I left my cell up there." Stupid decision but water and cell phones didn't mix. She should know. She'd knocked one into the shampoo bowl before and that had cost a pretty penny to replace. "With the storm moving on, I might be able to get through."

"Yeah."

As Cassie pulled at the passenger door, an iron grip manacled her wrist. She whipped around.

"What's your name?"

She stared down at his fingers. For a wounded man, he was strong! "I'm Cassie. What's yours?"

"What happened?"

There again the hint that he was more injured than he let on.

"You've had an accident." Gently she wiggled her wrist but he held fast. "What's your name?"

Not a bad idea to know in case he went unconscious again before emergency help arrived. You could never tell about head injuries.

"Monroe." Did his voice sound slurred? "Heath Monroe."

It fit him. Masculine. Strong. She tugged against his powerful grip. "You can turn loose now."

Slowly, he shook his head.

"Cassie." The way he said it sent a little tremor down her spine. He moistened his lips and swallowed. "Don't go."

His fingers went slack. Definitely addled.

"Hang tight, Heath, I'll be right back. Promise."

As good as her word, she was back in minutes. This time she'd tucked her cell phone inside a plastic shopping bag and brought it along. Just in case.

By the time she returned, he'd removed his seat belt and was rummaging in the console. The deployed air bag draped over his lap like an enormous melted marshmallow. Maybe that explained his confusion. An air bag packed a wallop.

She slammed the door, grateful to be inside again. The wet cold seeped into her bones.

"I made contact with my brother. He knows the area. He'll get help and bring them here."

The man's head dropped back against the headrest, eyes drifting closed. Whatever he'd been rummaging for was forgotten. He was still as pale as toothpaste. "Good."

"It could take a while. We're deep in the woods."

He rolled his head toward her. Beneath the dome light, his eyes were green like hers, though darker and more intense. The knowledge gave Cassie a funny feeling, as if they were connected somehow. "How far to Whisper Falls?"

Talking seemed to take more effort than it should.

"The town or the waterfall?"

"What?"

He was either addled or a total stranger to the area. "Whisper Falls is both a waterfall and a small town up here in the Ozarks. It's a long story but basically the town council decided to rename the town for the waterfall to attract tourists."

"And other things," he murmured, a statement which made her wonder all over again about his mental acuity.

"The falls is north of town, not far from where I live. The town itself is another six miles east. If you're headed to town, you missed the turn." Which made her wonder— why would a stranger be driving into Whisper Falls at this hour of the night?

Though the heater pumped out a warm hiss, it wasn't enough to penetrate the wet chill that had settled over her skin. Cassie shivered.

"You're cold."

"I'll live." She hugged herself, rubbing her hands up and down on her goose-bumped arms. She had a sudden memory of accident victims needing a blanket to keep from going into shock. Or something like that. There was no blanket available, but she had a suitcase full of clothes in the car. She could cover him with a sweater or two. "Are you warm enough?"

He didn't answer. He'd closed his eyes again and gotten quiet. Cassie fretted. Had his pallor increased? Was he asleep or unconscious? Remembering all the movies in which sleep was bad for a head injury, Cassie thought she should keep him talking. If there was one thing other than haircuts Cassie was good at, it was talking. "How's the leg?"

His eyelids fluttered but he didn't move otherwise. "Numb. Stuck. Frustrating."

"That's an understatement." She'd always been a talker, but years as a hairdresser had honed the skill. As her brother, Austin, often said, she could talk to a fence post. He should know. She talked to him, a man who'd rather have a stick in the eye as to carry on a conversation. "Do you hurt anywhere? Any other injuries you can determine?"

"A little headache."

"Little? Or one of those headaches where a burly construction worker is slamming your brains with a hammer?"

"Yeah. Rattled my brains." He drew in a shuddering breath, wincing at the effort. Something else hurt whether he acknowledged it or not. "Careless. I'm a better driver than that."

Now they were getting somewhere. An entire coherent thought.

Encouraged, Cassie pushed on. "Male pride. You sound like my brother when a horse throws him."

One corner of Heath's mouth moved the slightest bit as if he wanted to engage but didn't quite have the energy. "Cowboy?"

"Austin's a rancher. His place is a few more miles up this road and then back down a gravel road another mile and a half. Or did I tell you that already?"

"Boonies."

The comment was both apt and revealing. "Where are you from, Heath? Are you a city boy?"

He went silent again though Cassie was pretty sure he was conscious. It was as if he had to think about his answers. Either he'd had his memory knocked sideways or he was avoiding the question, something that made no sense.

The headache must be taking a toll on his thought processes.

Finally, as though his mouth was parched, he moistened his lips again and muttered, "Houston."

"Texas?"

He managed a wry glance, one eyebrow arched the tiniest bit. "Is there any other?"

Good. He was sounding better. Texans were a proud lot.

"Surprised, because I'm from Texas, too. Austin and I moved here from outside of Dallas. We've been here a long time, but Mom and Dad still live there. That's where I've been this week. A friend got married and I was in the wedding." She smiled a little at the memory of her old friend so much in love. She'd suffered a bite of the green-eyed monster, too, normal she supposed even though she never expected to fall in love again. "I did some shopping, ate Mama's cooking. Gained weight. Fun times."

That brought about as much response as kissing a mirror. She glanced at the clock on the dash, fretting again. Where was Austin? He should have been here by now. She was growing weary of trying to carry on a one-sided conversation with a disturbingly attractive, head-injured man during a pretty scary thunderstorm. But keeping him alert, or at least awake, was imperative. Wasn't it?

She should have paid more attention in first aid classes.

"I do hair," she said. Okay, that was lame, but what was she supposed to talk about to a total stranger who didn't give her much to work with? "I'm good at it, too."

Not that you could tell right now, with her straight black layers plastered flat against her head and dripping all over his leather interior.

"'Scuse me?" His eyelids lifted to half-staff. He had noticeably long lashes, thick and spiky, that shadowed his cheekbones. Thick eyebrows slashed above his eyes. No wax. She would know. She did plenty of wax jobs, even on men, though some of them swore her to secrecy.

"I'm a hairstylist. I do nails, too. My partner, Louise, and I run the Tress and Tan Salon in Whisper Falls." She wiggled her fingers at him. Her nails were acrylic, a tidy length but decorated with tiny tuxedoes in honor of the wedding. "Need a mani-pedi?"

His face was still too pale, but he managed a faint smile. More of a grimace, really, but an attempt to stay awake. "If I have any toes left."

Ouch. "My brother should be here soon. Don't worry. We'll get you out of here and that pedicure will be on the house. All ten toes."

"Optimist." The word had weakened, tapering off at the end so that it sounded more like 'optimisss.' Not good. *Come on, Austin.*

"Do you always drive off into strange places during raging thunderstorms? And why Whisper Falls? Visiting relatives?" When he didn't answer, she touched his arm. "Come on, Heath, stay awake."

"Late start." He was trying. She'd give him that much. "GPS...not too dependable."

"You got lost. Figures. Anyone can get lost out here." And he probably had been too proud and stubborn to stop and ask directions. Darrell had been like that, confident the location was right around the corner. "Mountains and trees are not impressed by modern technology."

He closed his eyes again, worrying Cassie. The car engine was still engaged, and a quick glance at the dash indicated plenty of gas. At least he'd had the presence of mind to fill up sometime in the recent past. They were warm and secure, the thunderstorm subsiding somewhat as it moved toward the east, though the rumbles continued and lightning flickered.

"Thunderstorms here are pretty spectacular. The noise echoes for miles." His cheek twitched but he didn't answer. Cassie reached for his pulse. "Are you still with me?"

"Yeah." The word was barely a whisper.

Was he bleeding internally? Going into shock? Cassie's mind raced, but all she could come up with were scenes from *General Hospital* and crazy words like *subdural hematoma.* Whatever that was.

The car grew silent. Cassie thought she should be doing something proactive but didn't know what. So she sat beside the injured man and chatted away about Whisper Falls and every single head of hair she'd ever groomed, praying that Austin and an emergency crew would get here soon. The man would know more about Whisper Falls than she did—if he could remember.

"Heath?" she said, shaking his shoulder.

His eyes fluttered up. Did they look more glazed now than before?

"You're pretty," he mumbled. "Got a boyfriend?"

Yes, he was delusional. Delirious. Poor man.

"No. My husband died."

"Sorry."

Not wanting to discuss Darrell's death, she shifted the topic to him. "What about you? Any significant other I should call? Girlfriend? Wife?"

"No more."

Okay, so he was either divorced or had recently broken it off with a girlfriend or worse, like her, his spouse had died. A curl of empathy circled through her. Being alone hurt. No matter how she'd tried to fill her life with activities, she missed the closeness of being a couple. She missed Darrell. In fact, she'd been missing him the day she'd climbed Whisper Falls. And guess what? Her prayer hadn't been answered. She was still laughing at herself over that silly episode.

"Who are you visiting in Whisper Falls?"

"Police chief."

"JoEtta Farnsworth?"

"Know her?"

His words were definitely slurring.

"Everyone in Whisper Falls knows Chief Farnsworth. Tough, fair and…eccentric to say the least. Are you related?"

The chief had kids somewhere but Cassie couldn't recall whether they were male or female or where they lived. One thing for certain, they didn't come around Whisper Falls too often. Heath's last name was different but that didn't mean much these days, and if Heath was the chief's son, he was a jerk of the first order for never coming to see his mother. JoEtta was gruff and rough but a good person.

Whatever the connection, Heath didn't answer. The car went silent again except for the endless drip of rain from the overhanging trees.

"Heath?"

He didn't move.

She touched him. "Heath."

He didn't respond.

"Come on, pal, stay with me. I don't like it when you take naps. It's not fair. You can't nap if I can't."

Heart in her throat, she grabbed his wrist, felt for a pulse. A thready beat pulsated against her fingertips.

"Heath, wake up. Talk to me."

He didn't.

Help needed to get here and it needed to get here now.

Chapter Two

Cassie pulled out her cell phone and tried again to reach her brother. She had one single bar of service but maybe that was enough. When Austin didn't answer, she punched in 911 once more. Before the call could connect, she heard the wail of a siren.

She almost melted in relief. *Thank You, Lord.*

"They're here, Heath." She patted his shoulder. "You'll be okay now. Hang tight. I'm going up to the road to direct them down to you."

She didn't know if the handsome stranger heard her or not, but she shoved the door open and raced up the steep incline, heedless of the brambles that were every bit as relentless on the ascent as they were coming down. Her breath came in short gasps as she tried to hurry.

She saw Austin's truck first and though light rain peppered her skin, she rushed toward her parked car and flipped on the headlights. Austin wheeled in next to her and leaped out of the truck.

"You okay?" Her tall, cowboy brother was a born protector.

"Soaked. Cold but all right. The guy in the SUV isn't doing so hot, though."

"You look like a drowned rat." Austin reached back inside the truck and pulled out a jacket, handing it to her. "Put this on."

Grateful for the warmth, she slid her arms into his oversize fleece.

About that time, the Whisper Falls's volunteer fire and rescue truck arrived. The crew varied, but tonight was not the usual group of volunteers. As the siren died away, Mayor Rusty Fairchild, a fresh-faced Opie look-alike hopped out of the cab in a warm-looking yellow slicker and rain boots, accompanied by Evangeline Perryman and paramedic Creed Carter.

The police chief pulled in right behind the rescue truck. Suddenly the dark night was bright with vehicle lights and people carrying brilliant halogen spotlights.

With a sense of profound relief, Cassie had never been so glad to see human beings in her life. People she knew and trusted. Good people, who made up in love and commitment what they lacked in fancy equipment.

"Where's the patient?" Creed Carter asked. She was especially glad to see Creed. The husband of her close friend Haley the chopper pilot was medic trained in the military and often ran medi-flights out of the mountains. He was cool as ice water in an emergency and always seemed to know what to do.

"Down there." She pointed her flashlight. "His leg is trapped. Not sure how bad, and I think he has a head injury. He was talking but—"

"Trapped?" Creed whirled toward Evangeline, a large, rawboned hill woman who lived with a pig. Literally. Cassie should know, she painted the pig's toenails for special occasions. "We'll need the ram."

The crew grabbed a tackle box of gear, a length of hose, and something that looked like a small generator and followed Cassie through the damaged brush and trees to the accident site.

In seconds the crew, along with Austin and JoEtta, swarmed the still-running SUV. Cassie realized she was shaking all over, an adrenaline flush, she supposed, in addition to the cold and wet. She wanted to climb back into the car with Heath and make sure he was all right but there didn't appear to be room. Evangeline was in the front seat, taking vital signs while Creed shined a penlight at Heath's pupils.

She wasn't needed now, though she'd developed an odd kind of bond with the stranger and was reluctant to leave. So she stood a few feet away, shivering, and watched as the rescuers did their work.

A boom of thunder shook the earth. Rain started to fall again, peppering her and the rescuers.

"Go to the car," Austin called, looking up from his spot next to Creed. The two men, both strong and fit, were wedging some sort of long, metal tool between the door post and the dash.

She wasn't leaving. Not until she knew Heath would be all right. They were in this thing together. And she owed him a pedicure. "Is he okay?"

"He's still with us."

That was something anyway.

"Did you call Moreburg for an ambulance?" The town of Whisper Falls had no hospital and had to depend on a nearby town or Creed Carter's helicopter for medical transport. She doubted he could fly in this storm.

"'Course I did." The police chief pushed away from the SUV where she'd been shining her light on the impact site and clumped to Cassie's side, gear rattling. Over fifty and gruff as a Rottweiler, JoEtta Farnsworth was a career police officer with more quirks than this road had curves. Dressed in her usual leather vest and brown boots, tonight she was minus the aviator goggles and helmet she normally wore on her scooter patrols through Whisper Falls. Instead, she'd wisely worn a flat-brimmed hat. "They may be a while."

"Creed can't fly in this weather."

"Nope. Don't worry, we've handled emergencies up here before. Problem though, we've got our hands full in town, too."

"What's going on?"

"Tornado touched down on the east edge."

"A tornado? Oh, no!" Remembering the violent thunderstorm, Cassie shouldn't have been surprised. "Is anyone hurt?"

"Got people out checking. State police will be along as soon as they can to help out. Mostly looks like trees and power lines down, but we won't know for a while, it being dark and all, and you never can tell for sure until daylight."

"Was there damage to any of the businesses?" Her shop was smack in the middle of the main street area.

JoEtta gave her a long look. "Don't know yet, missy. We're doing the best we can, and then this feller has to run his car off in a ravine."

"I'm sure he did it to annoy you, Chief."

JoEtta snorted. "I figure you're right. What happened here? Did you witness the accident?"

"I saw him lose control, saw his taillights spin away, but in the dark, I didn't see him leave the roadway." She shivered and huddled closer inside the jacket. Austin was right. Drowned rat.

"He was lucky you came along." The chief peered at the SUV, thinking. "Speeding?"

"I don't think so. The rain was a deluge and visibility was terrible. I think he probably didn't see the sharp curve until he was in it."

"Likely you're right. He wouldn't be the first." Rain trickled off her hat brim. "I didn't want to get in the way while they were doing the extraction but I stuck my head in. I didn't notice any alcohol or drug smells, did you?"

"No, nothing like that." The only smell she recalled was the cologne-scented air freshener dangling from his mirror. "He has a bump on his head." Suddenly remembering that important detail, she yelled, "Creed, check the left side of his head near the temple."

"Got it."

"Was he coherent enough to give his name? Any info about what he was doing out here? Anything at all to help with this investigation?"

In all the excitement, Cassie had forgotten. "He said he was on his way to Whisper Falls to see you. I thought he might be a relative."

"Me?" The chief's head spun to the accident and without another word, she stomped toward the SUV and the rough whine of a gas-powered generator. Metal screeched, a high-pitched sound worse than a fork on a plate, as the hydraulic ram slowly pushed the dash away from Heath's body.

Cassie clenched her back teeth against the noise, fighting a queasy fear about the man's leg. Praying the rescue wouldn't damage him more, she trotted to catch up with the police woman. "His name is Heath Monroe. Do you know him?"

"Heath Monroe is my new assistant chief," JoEtta barked, "*if* he hasn't gone and killed himself."

"Bust me out of here, Doc." Heath punched the end icon on his cell phone as the doctor, lab coat flaring out at the sides, breezed into the hospital room. Already this morning, Heath had touched base with Chief Farnsworth and run some digital errands, but being stuck in a Fayetteville hospital felt as confining as a Guatemalan jail cell. To his regret, he'd spent some time there, as well.

"In a hurry to get somewhere?" The doctor tapped a screen on his smartphone and stared at it while they talked. Heath wondered if he was playing fantasy football or reading Heath's medical reports.

"Yeah, I am." He was always in a hurry. Criminals didn't take days off.

Dr. Amil, a short, pleasant-looking physician with white at the temples, stashed the phone in his jacket and unwound a stethoscope from his neck, stuck the ends in his ears and pressed the cold end to Heath's chest. While he listened to whatever doctors listen for, he asked, "How's the head?"

"Terrific," Heath lied. The sucker throbbed with a dull ache and every time he sat up in this humiliating backless gown, he saw spots and felt nauseated. He'd had concussions before. He'd live.

"Any nausea or vomiting?"

Heath huffed. He wanted to roll his eyes but it hurt too much. "I'm all right, Doc. I've had worse. Bust me out of here. I have work to do."

As calm as if his patient wasn't fidgeting like a six-year-old in church, the doctor removed a penlight from his coat pocket and shined it in Heath's eyes. "Pupils reactive, equal." He straightened. "CAT scan was clear, no bleeding. You were lucky. Let's look at that ankle."

With a beleaguered sigh, Heath yanked the sheet from his left leg. He was more than lucky. As in all his other close calls, Somebody bigger than him was on duty. "Leg's just bruised, Doc. Slap a wrap on it and cut me loose."

Dr. Amil didn't seem in any hurry to comply. "Just because no bones are broken, doesn't mean you can get around on this leg, Mr. Monroe. The ligaments and tendons have been sorely stretched as you can tell by the deep purple bruising around the ankle and foot. PT will be up in a while to fit you with a boot."

Heath audibly groaned. "Please tell me this is a cowboy boot, custom made, fine cowhide. Otherwise, I'm good with a brace."

The physician chuckled in a flash of white teeth against a swarthy face. "Mr. Monroe, you're a stubborn man."

"I've been told that. I won't wear a boot, Doc. Sorry. Don't bother sending one up. Too bulky. Too restrictive. Bring me a wrap or a brace or something simple and I'll get out of your hair."

Dr. Amil studied him for a moment, hand to his chin, assessing. Heath always wondered what went on the mind of someone brilliant enough to be a doctor. Even Sam, his best friend from childhood, now an A-1 cardio-thoracic surgeon in Houston, was sometimes on a different wavelength than the rest of the world.

"You'll regret the decision unless you stay off this leg for a while. Two weeks at least with gradual weight bearing and activity."

"Understood."

"Your injuries are mostly minor, nothing rest won't cure. X-rays and CAT scan are clear, blood work is within normal limits. No need to keep you here any longer, especially since you have made up your mind to leave us." He offered a small smile. "But you *must* take it easy and give your body time to heal."

"Got it. Time heals all wounds." Which wasn't exactly true. Time hadn't healed some of Heath's deepest wounds. He'd come to grips with them and moved on, but healed? Not happening.

Troubled by his unusually morose thoughts and figuring he was more concussed than he wanted to admit, Heath squirmed, searching for a more comfortable position. In a hospital bed, he seemed to be constantly sliding downhill. The movement shot pain through his rib cage and ankle and set his head awhirl. Running off the road on his way to Whisper Falls had proven very inconvenient. "My new boss is coming to pick me up. Am I good to go when she gets here?"

He'd made a commitment and he planned to keep it even if he was twenty-four hours late and a little banged up.

"As soon as your paperwork is ready, but as I said, take life easy for a few days. No strenuous activity, no heavy lifting or sports. Avoid alcohol, sleep a lot, and you probably shouldn't make any important decisions for a few days. The nurse will give you a treatment sheet to take with you. It includes problems to look for. If any symptoms worsen, give us a call."

"Got it." He wasn't going to follow through, but he understood the message. Even though the hospital's overnight hospitality had been superb, he'd had all of it he could endure.

The minute the doctor exited the small room, Heath hobbled out of bed to get dressed. His head spun, making him lean against the wall until the fog cleared. With wry humor, he wondered if his eyes had crossed. To check, he leaned into the mirror for a look. His beard was scraggly. He rubbed a hand over it, wincing at how sore a man could be from a minor accident. After finding a plastic bag containing his clothes, he limped to the shower, eager to get rid of the humiliating gown. In the mirror, he gazed with fascination at the discoloration on his chest and shoulder. No wonder he was sore. The black eye was pretty entertaining, too.

Sore or not, he couldn't let this unexpected detour deter him from the job he'd been hired to do. He fumbled in the pocket of his jeans for the badge he'd carried every day since he was twelve years old. Running his fingertips over the now-dulled finish and the distinctive Lone Star in the center, he thought of the man who'd given his life to uphold everything this badge stood for. Heath was determined not to let him down.

By the time Chief Farnsworth crashed through the door like a battering ram, Heath had showered and dressed and was sitting in the regulation high-backed uncomfortable chair in the corner of the unit, completely exhausted and furious to be so. The shower had helped clear his head but it hadn't done much for his aching body.

"Heath Monroe, you're a heap of trouble. You better live up to your reputation."

He'd been warned that Chief Farnsworth was tough and blunt. "I plan to."

She stomped to his chair side and speared him with a long appraisal. "You look like you hit a tree."

"Feel like it, too."

"Ha! What's the doc say?"

"I'm free to go."

"You'll need a few days of R and R."

"No, I'm good to go."

The chief hackled up like a mad cat. "Don't argue with me, Monroe. You might be DEA, but I'm the officer in charge."

"Former DEA, Chief, but you're right. It's your town. I'm grateful you took me on." The slower pace of Whisper Falls was exactly what he wanted, at least for a while. They'd agreed to a six-month trial period, and after that, who knew?

"Feel lucky to get a man like you. Though I have to admit I wonder why you'd want to come to a boring, rural town to play second fiddle to someone like me. Frankly, I wondered if you'd show up."

"I'm a man of my word." He took a slow, easy inhale, testing the bruised ribs, proud to hold back a wince. "Boring and quiet sounds good right now."

"So you said. Burned out. Worn down."

Those might not have been his exact words but close enough. "Something like that."

"Well, you've come to the right place. We don't have much crime, though the rise in tourism has caused a few issues. There was a time I could handle everything myself with a couple of part-timers and the occasional auxiliary for special occasions, but lately…Well, I'm not getting any younger. Having a full-time, experienced assistant chief will take a load off." She spun a small, straight-backed chair close to his and plopped down. "Now. About you and this accident. You'll need a few days to get familiar with Whisper Falls and the surrounding area. Might as well use that as healing time. When you start prowling around town on duty, you'll need to be in top shape."

Heath figured his definition of top shape and the chief's were two different things. "How's my SUV?"

"I had it hauled in to Tommy's Busted Knuckle after we got you shipped up here last night. You'll have to talk to Tommy." She rubbed at her nose, sharp eyes still assessing him. "Cassie Blackwell saved your hide, son. We'd never have found you down in that hole if she hadn't seen you go off the road."

Cassie Blackwell. That was the name he'd been trying to remember all morning. "I owe her."

"Sure do. She's a good girl, our Cassie. You'll be seeing her around."

He hoped so. Even with a crack on the skull, he remembered Cassie. Silky voice, dark wet hair and huge eyes. Pretty. Really pretty. He wouldn't mind seeing Cassie Blackwell again. "She offered me a pedicure."

"What?" Chief looked at him as if he was still addled.

He shook his head, thinking he was still too fuzzy to make sense. "Nothing. Something funny she said to me last night. I think she was trying to keep me awake."

"That's Cassie. She can talk a blue streak."

He remembered that much. She'd talked on and on when all he'd wanted to do was sleep. He thought she may have told him her life story and that of every person in Whisper Falls—which could come in handy in his job, if he could remember.

"Where's that nurse?" The chief glared at the door, willing it to open. "We got to get moving."

Heath's head was pounding again. He really wished the chief wouldn't talk so loud.

She pointed at him. "Sit tight, Monroe. I'll go see if I can bail you out. The blasted rain finally let up, but we got us a mess in Whisper Falls, and the sooner we get back, the better."

He waited until the blustering chief charged out of the room. Then he took out his cell phone and dialed 411. Heath Monroe was a man who paid his debts. And he owed Cassie Blackwell.

Chapter Three

The morning was clear and sunny, a perfect spring day when daffodils burst from the damp earth to nod their golden heads and the wind is so still a stranger wouldn't believe how wild the sky had been last night. That is, until they arrived in downtown Whisper Falls and saw the mess.

Limbs and trash, asphalt shingles from someone's roof, trash cans and lids, and a smattering of kids' plastic toys were scattered down the streets and against business doors. The residential areas looked far worse. Cassie had even seen a doghouse hanging in a tree. She hoped the dog hadn't been in it.

Along with every other businessperson in town, Cassie had hit the streets at daylight to assess the damage. From the looks of things, nothing was completely destroyed, but they'd have plenty of cleanup to keep them busy for days.

She wiped the back of her wrist across her forehead, tired and oddly disheartened. She should be thankful, all things considered. Her shop was intact, her family and friends were safe, and even the stranger in the accident was reported to be in good condition.

She hadn't slept much last night, given the late hour she'd gotten home and the whirl of excitement that had gone on before. Heath Monroe had played around the edges of her mind even while she'd slept. She'd awakened after a reenactment of that long period when she'd been alone with him inside the crashed vehicle. She'd been afraid for him.

All night, she'd fought the temptation to call Chief Farnsworth for an update but had waited until this morning. The chief had her hands full with the aftermath of an F1 tornado and if Cassie knew JoEtta Farnsworth, the chief had slept less than anyone.

"Thank God the tornado was a little one," she muttered as she bagged trash and listened to the whine of chain saws. Her brother, Austin, Davis Turner and a group of other men manned the saws, clearing broken trees and limbs whereever needed.

"I'm thankful we didn't take a direct hit." This from Evelyn Parsons, the town's matriarch. The older woman, whose salt-and-pepper hair was kinked tight as corkscrews in the damp morning air, had literally put Whisper Falls on the map. She wouldn't take it lightly if the town was blown away after all her efforts to revive it. Miss Evelyn had turned a rumor into a tourist attraction. People came from all over to pray under the waterfall outside of town, hopeful that the rumor was true, that God really did answer prayers murmured there. In the opinion of Miss Evelyn and most of Whisper Falls, everyone benefited from the story and it never hurt to pray. The comment made Cassie feel a little better about her own pilgrimage, though she would be embarrassed if anyone knew. "Uncle Digger said the worst damage is east of town. There aren't many houses or people out that way."

"A few but they're scattered all over the hills."

Darrell's cousin lived east of town, though he was far up in the hills and back in the woods. She should probably call the man but he hadn't been too friendly after Darrell's death, as if he blamed her somehow for the loss. Truthfully, he'd never seemed to like her and they hadn't spoken since the funeral.

"Not likely any of them took a hit. The tornado dissipated not long after it moved over the town."

"True. I'm sure they're fine." Cassie peeled a soggy magazine from the side of a building and tossed it into the bag. "I have appointments this morning. Should we open for business?"

"Absolutely!" Miss Evelyn said. "This cleanup will take days, and that's why we pay city workers and have a strong corps of volunteers. The sooner we get back to normal, the better."

At eight, Cassie headed to the salon for a quick shower and change before her first appointment at eight-thirty. By ten o'clock the small salon was packed with customers and gossipers. Everyone knew there were two places in Whisper Falls to get all the latest news: Cassie's Tress and Tan Salon and the Iron Horse Snack Shop down at the train depot, run by none other than Miss Evelyn and Uncle Digger Parsons. Cassie figured both businesses were hopping today.

Midmorning, the newly engaged Lana Ross stopped by in her quest for newspaper stories. Wearing her usual cowboy boots and bling jeans, the former country singer looked petite and pretty, her dark brown hair curving softly against her shoulders.

"Mr. Kendle wants photos for tomorrow's edition," she said. "But I wanted to be sure everyone in here was all right before I start snapping."

That was so like Lana. After a rough start to life and a failed singing career in Nashville, she'd come home to Whisper Falls and met and fallen in love with widower Davis Turner. Cassie was happy for them. After all they'd both been through, they deserved happiness. And so did their children, a trio of adorable matchmakers.

"We're all okay," Louise said. A gamine-faced woman with a shock of striped mahogany hair she wore in a short rock star emo cut, Louise was a master stylist and a creative manicurist. No one in town did nails like Louise. At the moment, she was painting filler into Ruby Faye Loggins's acrylics. "What about you and Davis?"

"Nothing damaged except Paige's trampoline. It's hanging on the back fence with the net ripped off. But boy, was the weather scary for a while."

"I heard there was some damage out by the airport. Has anyone talked to Creed or Haley?" This from Ruby Faye.

"I did," Lana said. "Creed's helicopter is all right. A couple of pieces of sheet metal blew off and broke out a window on one of the small planes parked outside though."

"That's too bad."

"At least everyone seems to be safe so far," Lana said. "But I heard Cassie had quite an adventure last night."

Like satellite dishes seeking a signal, all heads rotated toward Cassie. As sweet as her customers were, they also liked the excitement generated by a tornado or a car accident or even a big storm. The buzz of fascinated energy was like electricity this morning. Frankly, it made her tired.

"Tell us, Cassie," Ruby Faye insisted, her eyes wide and eager for more stories to share at the bait shop she and her husband owned.

Before Cassie could open her mouth, volunteer firefighter Evangeline Perryman beat her to it, giving a recap of the rescue.

"He's good-looking, too, girls. My, my, my. He made my heart flutter." She clapped a hand against her generous chest.

"That was your angina, Evangeline." This wry statement came from Ruby Faye at the manicure station.

While the others chuckled, Evangeline insisted, "He was a hunk, wasn't he, Cassie? Dark and mysterious and tight muscles. Tell them. He was a hunk."

"Well, okay, he was pretty cute." Understatement of the year. Heath was, as Evangeline insisted, a hunk.

"Did you get his name? JoEtta said he was coming to work for her."

"Heath Monroe."

"Is he single? I have a single daughter, you know, and boy, would I love to marry that girl off."

Cassie wasn't about to go there. Heath's single status was his business. If the ladies of Whisper Falls wanted to stalk the poor man, she wasn't getting involved. She was having enough problems not thinking about him as it was. Eventually she would see him again. Would he remember her? And why should she care one way or the other?

Her thoughts went back to that moment last night when the rescue team had carefully lifted Heath from the car. He'd tried to stand on his own, insisting he was all right. His eyes had found her and in that instance, they'd made some sort of sizzling connection—right before he passed out.

"Cassie? Cassie?"

Cassie came out of her reverie to see the whole shop staring at her once more. She looked down at the head she was shampooing. How long had she been standing here in a fog?

"Oh, sorry, I was just—thinking. Did you say something?"

Evangeline slapped a beefy hand on her thigh and chortled. "I think Cassie's daydreaming about our new police officer."

"Don't be silly." Even if it was true.

Cassie wrapped a towel around Fiona's well-shampooed

head and righted the style chair just as the shop door opened. She finished the towel dry and reached for her tools.

"Flowers?" Louise squeaked, a hopeful sound that lifted on the end. "For who?"

Louise was happily married with a toddler but her husband, sweet as he was, was not Mr. Romantic. Louise longed for him to send her flowers or whisk her away on a picnic. Even though she dropped hints on a regular basis, he never had.

Conversation in the beauty shop ceased as the satellite heads rotated toward the florist hidden behind the vase of colorful tulips and gerbera daisies. Lan Ying, the tiny Asian owner of Lan's Flowers and Gifts, set the clear glass vase on Cassie's workstation.

"For Cassie," she announced with a sly grin, black eyes snapping with interest and humor.

"Me?" Cassie paused to stare in amazement, hairbrush in one hand and the silent blow dryer in the other. Fiona didn't seem to mind that Cassie was no longer working on her new style. She, too, stared in bug-eyed interest at the bouquet.

"Why, Cassie dear," Fiona said, "I think you must have an admirer."

Cassie laughed. "No chance."

She never received flowers. Well, unless you counted the ones her mom and dad sent for special occasions. Maybe that was it. She'd forgotten some important date. "Let me see the card."

She put the brush and dryer down with a clatter that sounded outrageously loud in the too-quiet room, and reached inside the sunny mix of yellows, pinks and purples.

"These are beautiful, Lan. You've outdone yourself," she said as she pulled the card from inside the tiny envelope.

Her pulsed ricocheted. *Oh. My. Goodness. He didn't.* Her face was hot as a flatiron.

"Who sent them, Cassie? Don't keep us in suspense."

"I can tell by her expression that it's a man," Evangeline smacked with no small satisfaction. "I told you so. Either Heath Monroe is a very grateful man, or Cassie has a beau."

Heath was still half out of his head. That could be the only explanation for this uncharacteristic behavior. He worked alone. He didn't get too involved or too close. His business—his former business—didn't allow it.

He didn't like crowds, either, and judging from the noise coming from inside, there was a big one.

Heath ran a hand over his brown button-down and hobbled toward the glass door. The salon was housed in an attractive old building with an upper-story balcony painted in a cheery red and trimmed in white. The glass front door proclaimed Tress and Tan Salon.

He had never been in a beauty shop in his life. But he was a man who paid his debts. Get in, get it done, get out. If he didn't fall over first. The chief was already badgering him about R and R. Probably because of that little dizzy spell he'd experienced in her office.

His ankle felt the size of an elephant and shot pain up his leg with every step. After dumping his gear at the furnished garage apartment, he'd collapsed on the couch for a couple of hours but upon awakening the familiar drive to be up and moving had taken over.

All right, Monroe, admit it. He was curious about Cassie Blackwell, curious to know if she'd gotten the flowers, and since he was going to be living in this town, at least for a while, he wanted to make nice with the locals.

Might as well open the glass door and go inside. He'd entered worse, scarier and far more dangerous places. A chorus of female laughter rang out. With a wry shake of his head, Heath thought, *Maybe*.

He pulled open the door and stepped inside. The first thing he noticed was the sudden reduction in conversation. The second thing was the smell. Really good shampoo. The kind that compelled a man to bury his nose in a woman's hair.

His well-trained eyes scoped out the place in seconds. Three workstations but only two were manned. Or womaned, as it were. Zebra-striped chairs, a mish-mash of hair fixing doodads and a gaggle of gawking females. And that smell. That overriding, delicious scent of all things female.

He cleared his throat. "You got the flowers."

Cassie Blackwell stood at one of the workstations. She'd turned toward the door when it had opened and now stood as if paralyzed, the mirror behind her reflecting the straight, choppy cut of her black, black hair.

Gorgeous. Last night, he'd thought she was pretty but his head had been too messed up to know anything for certain. Today, there was no doubt. His drippy-wet, shivering heroine from last night was a knockout.

"Why aren't you in the hospital?" she asked and he took note of the biggest green eyes he'd ever seen. Green, like his. Cool.

"They don't keep slackers."

Every woman in the room clucked and then a cacophony started that made his head ache worse.

"You're hurt."

"Look at his eye. Quite a shiner."

"Are you the new police officer?"

He replied to the last. "Yes, ma'am. Heath Monroe."

For some reason, this brought another round of clucking accompanied by sly looks at Cassie.

He felt a little weird being the object of all this attention. Weird but amused. In his particular role as an agent, he'd been required to keep a low profile. He'd have to get used to being out in the open.

"Nice to meet you, ladies," he said, forcing a smile that made his bruised eye hurt.

His comment was met with a round of introductions which he figured was a good thing. Getting to know the people in town would be as important to this job as it had been in covert operations.

But even as he carried on polite conversations with the women, cataloguing which one's husband ran the bait shop and which was a retired schoolteacher, and who was at the scene last night, it was Cassie his gaze kept coming back to. Medium height, she looked taller in bright red high heels that matched her equally red lipstick. If he put his arms around her, she'd hit him about chin-high in sock feet. The wayward thought startled him. He didn't know this woman, other than she'd been kind enough to help an injured stranger. Why was he stirred by the thought of Cassie, the hairdresser, in cozy little socks?

"Thank you for the flowers," she said in that same silky voice that had invaded his concussed dreams. "They're beautiful, but you really didn't need to go to all that trouble."

"If you hadn't come along…" He let the thought ride. No use going there. They both knew. "Glad you like them."

Before he could make the expected quick exit, the door behind him opened. He couldn't help himself. Years of watching his back had him turning to the side as yet another female entered the building. This one was pretty in the way of women who spend a lot of time and money on their looks. Dressed to kill in a pencil-slim skirt and stiletto heels, she was a well-groomed blonde, blue-eyed and thinner than he liked his women. Not that he'd focused much on women in the past decade. He liked the female gender—a lot—but in his line of work, personal relationships had taken a backseat. About the time things started to progress, he'd be shipped off to some dark corner of the earth. Which was just as well. He had a job to do and a vow to keep.

Automatically, he touched his pocket and felt for the badge resting against his thigh, a reminder of his life's mission and why he'd never settled down.

"Louise, I broke a nail," the newcomer announced in a voice that said a broken fingernail was a state of emergency. She held up an index finger and pouted. "Can you fix it for me right quick? Pretty please?"

The wild-haired Louise nodded. The manicurist reminded him of those wide-eyed dolls whose heads were bigger than their bodies. "Sure thing, Michelle. Give me a couple of minutes to finish Ruby Fay."

"I have an appointment at the bank in a few—" The woman's voice trailed off when she spotted Heath. "Oh, my gracious, I am so sorry for interruptin'." She stuck out the hand with the broken nail. "I'm Michelle Jessup. You must be our new police officer."

Might as well get used to it. In a small town news carried far and fast.

"This is Heath Monroe, Michelle," Cassie said, taking up the tools of her trade again. "And you guessed right. He's our new assistant chief."

"My goodness gracious, Heath, honey, you are all beat up. Oh, this is terrible. Not a good welcome to our little burg at all." She pressed long-nailed fingers to her chest in an affected pose. Most of the people Heath had encountered so far in Whisper Falls spoke with a stronger-than-Texas accent but this woman's suddenly thickened to Southern syrup. "I heard about that scary accident you had. What a blessing our little Cassie came along in the nick of time."

Heath shot an amused look at "our little Cassie," who lifted one eyebrow but didn't speak. Heath didn't like to judge a person on first impressions, but Michelle was making a strong one.

"Very lucky. I could have been stuck down there for days before anyone found me."

"Well, isn't she just heroic?" Michelle gushed, moving into Heath's space with a flirty smile. "Your poor eye. It must hurt like crazy." She was close enough that he could smell her perfume, an exotic blend of flowers and spice. "My daddy owns Jessup's Pharmacy right down the street. If you need anything at all, you tell Daddy I sent you, and he'll fix you right up."

"I appreciate the offer. Thanks." He eased a step back.

"You are so welcome," Michelle said brightly, letting the last word trail off in a long, slow drawl. "Glad to help in any way I can. We take care of our people around here."

"We sure do," Louise muttered. "Especially our handsome new law-enforcement personnel."

A snicker ran around the edges of the room, but if Michelle noticed, she didn't let on. Heath practiced his poker face.

"I heard about your SUV being all smashed up. I am so sorry. If it can't be fixed and you have to have a new one, you come right on over to the bank and see me. As the chief loan officer in Whisper Falls, I will take *good* care of you."

A man would have to be blind, deaf and brain-dead not to get the message, though the woman couldn't know Heath was immune. He'd been propositioned by some of the best, usually when he was about to haul them to jail.

"Good to know. Appreciate it. Everyone here has been very helpful."

"Oh, Heath, you are so welcome." She tilted her head and hunched one shoulder in a pretty pose, flashing him a dazzling smile.

"Michelle, I'm ready for you." Louise patted the tabletop and motioned toward the chair. "Come on over. You don't want to be late for that appointment."

The flirtatious woman turned her back and walked toward the manicurist, hips swaying. Heath purposely glanced away, catching Cassie's eye. If he wasn't mistaken, she'd found the exchange as over-the-top as he had. Big green eyes dancing above some woman's haircut, she fawned and mouthed, "Oh, Heath."

Heath felt his nostrils flare as he fought back a laugh. Time to hit the road. He lifted a hand in farewell. "See you later."

Cassie tilted her head and smiled. "Thanks again for the flowers."

Their gazes held for several more seconds while he recalled the feel of her soft hands scanning his face and his hair. A zing of energy sizzled through him like last night's lightning.

Puzzling over the unexpected reaction to his rescuer, Heath limped out into the sunlight, the noise of female conversation trailing him. Once the coast was clear, he paused. Hands on his hips, he looked up into the sunny blue sky and laughed.

He wasn't sure what he'd signed up for, but Whisper Falls might turn out to be a lot more interesting than he'd ever expected.

Chapter Four

Thunderstorms had brewed up every afternoon for the entire week Heath had lived in Whisper Falls. The ground was a mud bog, delaying tornado cleanup. With the chief as his guide, he had spent the days cruising the town in their one and only police vehicle, getting acquainted. The citizens welcomed him with warmth and curiosity, commiserating over his wrecked SUV, his black eye and the ankle that refused to stop swelling like an overheated helium balloon.

Late Thursday morning, he propped said foot on a padded chair next to the scarred desk in what was now his official office—a closet-size cubicle beside the courthouse jail. A window looked out on the courthouse lawn, a pretty space with a Vietnam memorial marker, a statue of the town's founder and lots of springtime green. On the adjoining streetcars tooled past with slow irregularity. Easy Street was well named. Life was definitely slower here than anywhere else he'd been in a while. Not counting a tiny Mexican village that had once been his base for a very long three months.

He reached down and loosened the boot lace from around the yellow-and-purple ankle. Didn't hurt as much today, but the tautly stretched tissues were uncomfortable and he couldn't shake the limp. His head was clearer, though, thank the Father. Damage could have been a lot worse if not for Cassie Blackwell, though he wondered about the inordinate amount of time he'd spent thinking about the woman who'd saved his hide on a rain-slicked mountain road. So far, he'd resisted another trip to her sweet-smelling, female-fixing salon—a male's purgatory—but he wouldn't mind seeing Cassie again.

"Already laying down on the job, Monroe?" With her usual rowdy entrance, Chief Farnsworth slammed into this office. No knock. No warning. Just bam! "Wimping out over a measly dab of ankle pain?"

Heath gave her a lazy smile. "That's me. Any excuse not to work."

"Figures. You Feds are all the same. All blow and no go."

"And all you small-town Southern cops are corrupt." He crossed his arms over his chest. "Where'd you hide the body, Chief?"

Farnsworth barked a laugh. She was a straight-up law enforcer and Heath liked her. Didn't mind working for her, either. He'd never chaffed at having a woman superior officer. Watching his mother raise three boys alone had taught him the value, strength and leadership of the female gender.

She leaned a hand on his desk. "One of us needs to do a safety walk through the school and look for security weaknesses this afternoon. You up to the task?"

Heath pushed back from the desk. He never figured himself as a desk man and didn't plan to be much longer. Paperwork gave him colic. "Has someone made a threat?"

"No. Don't plan to have any, either, but if they come, we want our kids protected."

"You got that right. I don't mind the trip, a good excuse to get acquainted with school personnel." And hang with the kids. He missed his rambunctious nephews and that one fluffy-haired niece who could wrangle anything out of him with a dimpled smile.

"Sure you're up to it? Requires some walking around the campus."

Heath laced his boot, ignoring the throb and the question. "Want to call the superintendent? Or should I?"

"I'll call, give him fair warning. His name is Gary Cummings. Reserved, suit-type feller but sharp as bear teeth."

"Got it." He dropped his foot to the floor and winced. Annoying. "I need to stop by the garage and check on my truck. That all right with you?"

"Fine. I'm headed up to talk with Judge Watson. The county DA is here today to go over some charges. Why don't you cruise through town and make sure the citizens are behaving themselves?"

Heath huffed softly. "Is there any doubt? The place is quieter than a tomb." *Quiet* seemed too mild a word. He-could-hear-his-hair-grow quiet.

"Just you wait, mister. Storm's got 'em busy, but summer's coming. Things heat up."

He'd believe it when he saw it.

Eager to be doing anything other than sitting behind the desk, Heath was out the door and in the cruiser as fast as his bad ankle would take him. He liked Whisper Falls and had longed for peace and quiet. Be careful what you pray for, he supposed. In his former job, he'd rarely had a quiet day and the lack of action was making him a little crazy.

He cruised the streets first, eyes alert for anything out of the ordinary. So far this week, he and the chief had rousted a truant teenager, ticketed Bert Flaherty for doing forty in a twenty, responded to a possible dog theft and three domestics. Beyond that were the basic patrols, civic responsibilities and a handful of false alarms. He was still trying to figure out why Chief Farnsworth needed an assistant.

At the end of Easy Street, he pulled into Tommy's Busted Knuckle Garage to check on his ride.

Tommy, a long, skinny man with brassy shoulder-length hair and a wooly reddish beard met him in the bay. "How's the leg?"

"Good. What's the verdict on my SUV?"

Tommy scratched his beard. "Insurance adjuster was here this morning. Sorry to tell you, Heath, but she's a goner."

Heath grimaced. He'd been afraid of that. "I'm going to have to get a new one?"

"Looks that way."

He had a sudden vision of limping into the bank to ask Melissa Jessup for a loan, of having her pout over his poor little eye and his poor little ankle and his poor little broken car. Hiding a smile, he thought that might not be a bad thing. A man could use some feminine sympathy now and then.

Tommy clapped him on the shoulder and shook his shaggy head. "A rotten shame, a nice set of wheels like that, but I can't put her back the way she was."

He'd been fond of that SUV.

A rumble of thunder sounded in the distance. The men turned their heads toward the sound. Were they due for another storm this afternoon?

"Thanks anyway, Tommy. It was good of you to go out in the boonies and haul it up out of that ravine."

"Ah, no big deal. Just glad it was the truck that bit the dust instead of you."

"Can't argue that."

As he left the garage and started down Easy Street, he spotted a jaywalker. Not that he was going to ticket anyone for the infraction, but this jaywalker caught his attention. Glossy black hair that swung against her shoulders as she bopped along, a hot pink and zebra-printed smock over black pants and a pair of black high-heeled ankle-breakers.

His boredom vanished faster than chips at a dip tasting contest.

He whipped the car into a U-turn and parked at an angle in front of Evie's Sweets and Eats. He pressed the window button and watched the smoked glass slide away just as Cassie stepped up on the curb.

"'Morning," he said.

She pivoted toward him with a smile. "Hi. Except it's nearly noon."

"Yeah." He grinned.

"How are you?"

Better now.

"Healing." He touched the bruise over his left cheekbone. "How's it look?"

"Awful." But her smile softened the word. "Maybe you should run by the bank and get Melissa to feel sorry for you."

"I've been thinking about that."

"You have?"

"My vehicle is a goner. Gotta buy a new one."

"Oh, that's too bad." She stepped off the curb to stand by his car window. A flirty breeze ruffled her heavy bangs and he was pretty sure he smelled that fancy shampoo again.

Jockeying for a better view, Heath leaned an elbow on the window opening and tilted his face. Cassie had something that appealed to him. A kind of chic wholesomeness mixed with Southern friendly and a dash of real pretty. "Think I should get a loan from Melissa?"

Cassie grinned. "She's good at her job, if you can deal with the fact that she thinks you're the hottest thing to hit Whisper Falls since Pudge Loggins's turkey fryer caught fire and burned down his garage."

He hiked an eyebrow, amused and flattered and knowing very well what she meant. "Does she now?"

This time Cassie laughed, her scarlet mouth wide beneath dancing green irises. "Haven't you noticed the number of times she's been to the courthouse this week?"

He hadn't. Man, he must be losing his radar. He hitched his chin toward the bakery. "Were you going in there?"

"Lunch. Want to come? Evie makes good sandwiches from her own homemade bread. Fresh baked this morning."

"Best invitation I've had all day." Since he'd been here actually. The school didn't expect him for another hour, so he radioed his location to dispatch and exited the car. The ankle screamed at the first step, causing an involuntary hiss that infuriated Heath.

Cassie paused, watching him. "You're still in pain."

"No, I'm fine."

She made a disbelieving noise in the back of her throat. "You remind me so much of my brother."

"Must be a great guy."

She took the statement as the joke he'd intended. "The best. You should meet him."

"I'd like that."

"Come to church Sunday and you will."

Heath reached for the antique door handle. The scroll on the amber glass was equally antique as was the rounded arch transom above the door shaded by a red fringed awning.

"If I'm not on duty, I might do that." He needed a church, not that he'd ever had time to attend much, but he believed, and church was important in a small town.

With his ankle throbbing, he somehow held the door open for Cassie and limped inside a small business that smelled better than Grandma Monroe's kitchen on Thanksgiving. Though he wouldn't be sharing that information with Grandma. The smells of fresh breads and fruit Danish mingled with a showcase of pies and homemade candies.

"A cop's dream," he muttered, only half joking.

A middle-aged woman—Evie, he supposed—who obviously enjoyed her own baking, created their orders while maintaining a stream of small talk with Cassie. When she put his sandwich in front of him along with baked chips and a glass of tea, she said, "This one's on the house, Mr. Monroe, and dessert of your choice. Welcome to Whisper Falls."

"I can't let you do that."

"You don't have a choice. Go sit down and eat." She smiled. "And enjoy."

"Don't argue with her, Heath. Trust me, she'll get her money back from you." Cassie took the lunch tray before he could and led the way to a table. There were only three and all had a sidewalk view.

"Chief called me a wimp today. I'm starting to feel like one."

"How bad is your leg? I mean really. No bluffing. Any other injuries besides that?"

"Just the ankle. Sprained. And a couple of bruises here and there." Bruises that ripped the air out of his lungs. "Annoying. But I still have all ten toes." He bit into the thick, fragrant sandwich.

"I'm relieved to hear it. When do you want your mani-pedi?"

Heath choked, grabbed for the tea glass and managed to swallow. "My what?"

The thought of Cassie touching him again gave him a funny tingle. A nice tingle, come to think of it. Did she have any idea the thoughts that go through a man's head at the most inappropriate times?

"You don't remember our conversation?" she asked. "Is the concussion still bothering you?"

"Slight headache if I get tired. Nothing to worry about."

"Are you following up with Dr. Ron? He's a really good doctor." She pinched a piece of lettuce from her plate, holding it between finger and thumb. "And the only one in town."

"Next week."

"He's terrific. You'll like him." She nibbled the lettuce and then bit into the sandwich packed with vegetables and turkey. Between bites, she chattered about plans for a community storm cleanup, the Easter sunrise service at the Baptist Church—which she deemed "not to be missed" though Easter was several weeks past—and filled him in on the small, useful details of Whisper Falls.

"Some of this sounds familiar," he said after a long, cool drink of sweet tea. "Did you tell me this in the car?"

"I thought you didn't remember."

He never said that. He remembered bits and pieces. Like her silky voice and dogged efforts to keep him awake. "It's starting to come back to me."

"I've talked enough about Whisper Falls anyway. No use repeating myself again. Tell me about you. You're from Texas, not married, no kids. Any other family back in Texas?"

"Two brothers and a terrific mom."

"No sisters? Your poor mother."

"She had her hands full."

"I imagine so! Tell me about the brothers. Older or younger? What do they do?"

"Holt and Heston. Both younger. Both in law enforcement. Sort of. Holt is a private investigator. Heston's a street cop."

She tilted her head in a cute way that bunched her hair on her shoulder. He spotted a small sparkly earring. "Did they follow big brother's path or is law enforcement in the genes?"

"In the genes, I guess. My dad was a cop." His hand went to his pocket, to Dad's badge. "A great cop. He died in the line of duty."

Her perky expression fell. "That's awful, Heath. I'm sorry."

"Long time ago. Now we Monroe boys do our best to keep the bad guys off the streets." He faked a grin. Time to move this conversation to softer ground. "Tell me about you. Besides making the women of Whisper Falls beautiful, what do you do?"

She returned his grin, though hers said she knew he was changing the subject and empathized. She was a nice woman.

As he chewed his ham and provolone, Heath recognized that he was sharply drawn to Cassie Blackwell, to her bright mouth and alabaster skin. His reaction puzzled him. She was friendly to the max, but didn't flirt, yet Heath found her astonishingly attractive. Pulse-bumping attractive. Not that he worried about it much. He was accustomed to fast, brief relationships that went nowhere. Whether from duty or boredom, his interest in Cassie would burn out like the rest.

Cassie dipped the paintbrush into a tray filled with baby-blue color while her sister-in-law, Annalisa, worked her way around the small bedroom with a roll of masking tape and a straight edge, making sure every vertical stripe on the nursery wall was perfect.

A slight breeze drifted in the open window, a natural ventilation source, though Cassie had set a box fan in the doorway to help extract the paint fumes. The fan also kept the pack of dogs, particularly her apricot poodle, out of the way—much to Tootsie's annoyance. Even now, the spoiled mutt lay in the hallway, gazing in with a wounded expression.

Cassie had offered to paint the room alone, but Annalisa had insisted on helping. After all, this was her baby, her project, but working together was fun. Cassie was grateful to her sister-in-law for allowing her to be part of transforming the old guest room into an adorable nursery for her brother's baby. It was something she'd never get to do otherwise. Like her marriage, the dream of babies had died with her husband.

"The walls are looking gorgeous, Cassie." Annalisa sat back on her heels, blond ponytail dangling, to admire their handiwork. Latte-brown already covered the upper half of the nursery and now they were striping the bottom in latte and blue. White chair rail divided the upper from the lower, and white enamel trimmed the windows, doors and the bottom of the wall. "Everything looks so crisp and clean. I can't wait to put up the moon and star decor. Won't it be pretty?"

Cassie rolled her tired neck and smiled softly at her beautiful sister-in-law and dear friend. "No prettier than the stars in your eyes."

"Your brother—" Annalisa pushed a stray lock of hair behind her ear and sighed, one of those romantic, madly-in-love sounds that said more than words. "Who could imagine I'd end up on a ranch with a cowboy where I'm so happy I pinch myself every day to be sure it's real? I really love him, Cassie. More now than ever."

Annalisa's devotion to Austin never failed to warm Cassie. Her brother had been through a terrible time with his emotionally disturbed first wife, and she'd despaired of ever seeing him embrace life and love again. But a lost and abused woman in the woods and a whispered prayer had changed him.

"You make him happy, too, Annalisa."

"I know. That's the beauty of true love. We're both blessed, but I think I am most of all." She rubbed a palm over her basketball belly. "Finding Austin was the best thing that ever happened to me. And having our little cowboy pretty soon is a wonderful bonus."

Annalisa was one of those pregnant women who glowed. Her skin was clearer, her blue eyes brighter, and other than an intermittent battle with her blood pressure, she was full of energy. The ranch house had never been this clean! Not that housework was ever Cassie's gig. She'd rather have her toenails removed. Annalisa, on the other hand, thrived on making a house a home.

"Only a few more weeks and I'll be an aunt." Something odd twisted in her chest.

"Aunt Cassie." Annalisa cocked her head. "I like that."

"Me, too." The odd pulling came again, heavy and uncomfortable. She was delighted to be an aunt. Wanted to be aunt. Couldn't wait to hold her precious nephew.

If Darrell had lived they would have had a baby by now. Maybe two.

She turned back to the wall, carefully adding another stripe.

"You're better at that than I am."

Cassie snorted. "Painting stripes on walls is easier than painting designs on fingernails."

"I guess it would be." Annalisa went to the window and took a deep breath as she gazed out on the forest and mountain vista beyond the pasture land. Cassie was glad to see her go for some fresh air. "Everything is gorgeous and green this year."

"Thanks to the rain. It's been a couple of years since we had good spring rains." Cassie went back for more paint.

"I was starting to think I'd brought Texas drought with me to the Ozarks."

"The thunderstorms make me nervous. I'll be glad when they stop." Annalisa turned from the window, tummy leading.

"Me, too. The town has a lot of cleanup to do, and wild wind and rain every evening isn't helping."

"How was your lunch with the new policeman?"

Cassie lowered the paintbrush. "How did you know about that?"

"This is Whisper Falls, Cassie. Every single woman in town has her eye on Heath Monroe, and when he has lunch with one of them, it's big news." She put a hand to her back and arched, stretching, an action that made her belly huge.

"I don't have my eye on Heath. Or anyone else." Cassie carefully placed the brush across the top of the paint can. Plastic drop cloth crinkled as she pivoted on her old, paint-splattered canvas shoes.

Annalisa ambled to her paint tray. "Nothing wrong with being interested, Cassie. He's single, seems nice and needs to make friends."

"We ran into each other by accident. He's new in town and you know me, the welcome committee. I invited him to church to meet you and Austin."

Eyes on the paint, Annalisa dipped her brush and dragged the bristles along the tray top. "Aren't you the least bit interested?"

Was she? "I like him, if that's what you mean. He has a wicked sense of humor."

She liked his strength, too, and the way he downplayed his injuries when he could easily have taken advantage of the chief and done nothing for a few weeks. "Did you know his dad was a cop, too, and he died in the line of duty?"

"How sad for him." Annalisa lay the brush down to massage her belly with both hands.

Cassie wondered if the baby was moving. Wondered what it would feel like to have a baby growing inside. "I thought so, too."

"What's he doing here, in Whisper Falls? I mean, why here? Does he have family nearby?"

"I didn't ask."

"That's not like you."

"Don't worry, Michelle Jessup will find out for you."

"Probably so. She was in the Iron Horse this afternoon."

Oh, good grief. "Was that how you found out about our lunch?"

"She saw you and Heath come out of Evie's together." Resting on her knees beside the paint tray, Annalisa flashed a grin. "She thought you looked very cozy. The two of you were laughing."

Cassie frowned. "What's wrong with laughing?"

"You know Michelle. She was buzzing about our poor injured and oh-so-handsome policeman." Annalisa put her splayed fingers against her chest in an imitation of the banker and drawled. "She sincerely hoped poor, lonely Heath didn't let Whisper Falls's man-hungry females eat him up."

Cassie rolled her eyes. "Poor Heath is right. I like Michelle, but sometimes her daddy's-perfect-darling brattiness shows through the polished veneer. She can be a tad pushy."

"Doesn't hurt that Heath is very easy to look at." Annalisa hunched her shoulders and grinned impishly, blue eyes widening. "Don't tell Austin I said that."

"Tell Austin what?" At the male voice, both women looked toward the door. After a pat to the poodle's head, Austin stepped over the box fan.

"Nothing important, darling. Girl talk."

Cassie reached for a rag to wipe paint from her fingers, amused. "She's throwing you over for the new cop in town."

"Grrr." Austin's upper lip curled. "And here I thought I might like the guy. Now I have to beat him to a pulp."

Knowing he teased, Cassie tossed the paint rag at him. It bounced off his chest. "Down, tiger. She's all yours."

"Yes, I am." Annalisa waddled over and lifted her face toward his. The cowboy was considerably taller and broader than his leggy wife and his darkness contrasted with her fair hair. They were a beautiful couple. If Cassie didn't love them both to pieces, she'd be jealous.

"Nobody can take your place," Annalisa said, moving close until her belly bumped his. As Cassie looked on, Austin cupped the mound that held his child. With an aching tenderness, the pair shared a long, loving look before Austin bent his head and kissed his wife.

Cassie glanced away, busying herself with the cleanup. She loved them. She was glad for their happiness. But lately…

After comfortably sharing a home with her brother and sister-in-law for nearly two years, she was beginning to feel like a fifth wheel.

Chapter Five

"Ankle's still giving you trouble. Take time off and see a specialist."

"It's fine. I'm healing." Through sheer force of will, Heath refused to limp the four feet from the doorway to Chief Farnsworth's desk.

"Don't con me, Monroe. I saw you coming across the parking lot. You limp like a dog with a wooden leg."

"It's only been a couple of weeks. I'm all right. Now, what's this deal we're going to at noon?" He didn't care a bit where they were going but a change of topic was in order. His ankle was not a big deal. His job was.

"City planning committee. They want to meet you, for one thing. For another, they want our input on security for the new park they're hoping to build out near the waterfall." Chief went to the coffeepot. "Want some?"

Creed raised a hand. "I'm good. Thanks."

"Creed Carter called this morning." The gurgle of coffee sounded against the ceramic cup. "He flies scenic tours over the Ozarks. You met him at the accident scene."

A misty memory of that night floated somewhere in the back of his mind. "Saw him at church yesterday, too. Nice guy."

He'd seen a number of other people—including Austin Blackwell and his very pregnant wife—thanks to Cassie with her big warm smile and easy welcome. His eyes had zoned in on her the moment he'd limped through the double doors into the foyer and seen her chatting with Miss Evelyn Parsons. Then she'd invited him to sit with her and her brother, an offer he couldn't refuse. He'd liked the service all right, but mostly he'd liked seeing Cassie again.

"Are you paying attention, Monroe?"

"Sure thing, Chief. You said Creed spotted something out of the ordinary on a chopper tour this morning."

"Huh. Don't know how you do that. Zone out and still get the drift of my conversation."

"Skills, Chief." He shot her an ornery grin. "Must be the Fed in me."

The federal-versus-local jibes had become a regular part of their conversation. She was usually one up. Now they were even, though he had no doubt she'd zing him again real soon.

"Ha!" She dumped a little tub of creamer into her coffee and tossed the container in the trash. The can was starting to overflow. "I think we should check out the scene. Even though no one has said a word about any home losses from the tornado, we don't always get the complete news from the outlying areas."

"Did Creed get coordinates? We'll need to check to see if the area has been occupied. I'd hate to think someone was under a pile of debris for this long."

"You and me both. I'm going to take a run out there. Think you can handle things here?"

He'd much rather take a drive to the country. "Got it. Let me know if you need assist."

Forty-five minutes later, Chief Farnsworth was on the phone. "Monroe, better get out here."

"What's going on? What did you find?"

"We'll talk when you get here. Alert dispatch and head this way."

He'd no more than hung up when it hit him. Chief Farnsworth had taken the cruiser. He didn't have a vehicle.

The chief was laughing at him as Heath rattled to a stop alongside a mobile home—or what appeared to have been a mobile home. A pile of sheet metal, furniture and debris was scattered in an irregular pattern beneath a stand of broken trees.

Heath slammed out of the dented, rusty old truck and strode with the smallest limp possible toward his guffawing boss.

"Forgot about the vehicle issue. That's what happens when you work alone too long." She adjusted her sunglasses, a pair of goggles straight out of the Amelia Earhart era. "Where did you get that old truck?"

"Tommy at the Busted Knuckle. I rented it from him."

"Resourceful."

"You'll get a bill for it."

Her bark of a laugh caused a pair of cardinals to take flight. "You need your own truck. City pays mileage and upkeep. Take off tomorrow and get one."

"Works for me." His eyes had been taking in the scene all during the chitchat time. "Looks like the tornado hit here. Either that or a meth explosion."

"Funny you'd say that. Come over here by the A/C unit and see what you think of this."

Following her lead, Heath picked his way across the mounds of trash, thankful no dead body had been discovered in the ruins. Trash, papers, clothes, food containers were spread everywhere, even into the nearby trees. Ap-

pliances and furniture had been ruined either by the storm
or the elements.

"What do you make of these?" With a snap, the chief
donned rubber gloves and went to her haunches, indicating a ripped trash bag and its contents.

An adrenaline chill prickled Heath's skin. "That looks
familiar."

"Thought it might." She tossed him a pair of gloves.
"Let's bag it up and take it in for analysis, but I'd bet my
badge we'll get a positive hit for drugs."

"Cocaine." Carefully, he pushed the debris aside with
the toe of his boot. "An unusual amount of baking soda to
keep on hand, wouldn't you say?"

"Think they were cooking crack?"

Her reply surprised him only a little. Remote areas
were often the heart of illegal drug operations simply because they were hard to police. Even though Whisper Falls
seemed Mayberry perfect, Chief had probably run into her
share of druggies.

"Looks that way," he replied. "If we poke around, we'll
probably find other paraphernalia—unless they took it with
them."

"I guess you've seen plenty enough to know."

Grimly, Heath lifted one of the bags, noting the telltale
markings. Drug cartels marked their packages, though he
didn't recognize this particular brand. "Way too many."

"So the fellows that lived out here were likely dealers."
Chief used a stick to carefully rummage for more evidence.
An investigator never knew when a dirty needle might
catch her off guard.

"Or smugglers who brought in the powdered cocaine,
cooked it into crack and then moved it to their army of dealers." He leaned close and sniffed. Too much rain had eradi-
cated the smell. "Do you know who lived here?"

"Man name of Louis Carmichael. Kept to himself, none too friendly, didn't come into town much."

"Appears he had a reason for keeping a low profile."

"This is more your area of expertise than mine," the chief said. "Tell me what you think."

"Let's go through the debris and see what else we find. I want to know who brought it in, where it came from, where it was headed. If they were packaging and selling from here or distributing elsewhere. Lots to consider." Heath pushed to his feet.

"You'll take the lead on this." It wasn't a question.

Heath parked his fists on his hip bones. The badge in his pocket was like a flaming thing, a warm and ever-present reminder. He'd wanted a break from the war on drugs, but he had a commitment, too. He'd take the lead, all right, and he'd track down the slimeballs who'd killed his father. Maybe not the exact person, but all who dealt in the drug trade were guilty. And he was the man to bring them to justice.

The next morning Heath stopped in at Evie's Sweets and Eats for a coffee and Danish before his trek to the Fayetteville car dealership. Cassie was right. Evie was quickly earning back the cost of her welcome lunch. Add Evie's homemade bread to the bonus of seeing Cassie here on several occasions and he was becoming a regular.

As he pulled open the door, Heath glanced across the street toward the Tress and Tan. Cassie's shiny green Nissan wasn't in the usual spot.

With a curious frown, he went inside. Where was she? Sick? He'd never known her to run late. The salon lights came on by eight-thirty every morning and didn't shut off until after six. He knew. Just as he knew the routine of every other business in town. Knowing was his job.

"'Morning, Heath," Evie called, her full face pink with exertion, as she lifted trays of fragrant pastry into the display cases. "May I help you?"

He cast another frown toward the salon. "Has Cassie been in yet? Her car isn't there."

"Cassie?" Evie ran a dry cloth along the front of a windowed display. "This is Wednesday. She's never there on Wednesday or Sunday. Her days off. You asking for a reason?"

"No. No. Just curious. She's always so…punctual."

"Punctual." Evie smiled and tossed the polish cloth onto the counter behind her. "That she is. Now what can I do for you, Heath?"

"Fortify me for a day of truck hunting. I'm headed to Fayetteville. Coffee to go and a couple of those cherry Danish."

"I saw you driving Tommy's old beater."

"Nice of him to rent it to me."

"Skinflint should have loaned that old dog to you." She poured an extra large serving of coffee, capped it, and pushed the disposable cup toward him. "Who's going with you?"

"Nobody but me."

Her eyebrows shot halfway to her widow's peak. "How are you going to get two vehicles back to Whisper Falls?"

With the fragrant scent of good coffee tickling his nose, Heath stared at the woman for two beats. She was right. He needed an extra driver.

The concussion must have been worse than he'd thought.

The phone call from Heath Monroe had been unexpected but when she'd heard his plight, she knew the request had nothing to do with her in particular. He didn't know many people in town. She was available. He needed a favor—someone to drive. That's what friends were for.

And frankly, the call had come at the best possible time. She'd been cornered at the post office listening to Mr. Pierce rant about politics and the cost of living. Not that she didn't hear this particular topic on a regular basis at the shop, but there she got paid to listen. And Mr. Pierce had a way of loudly spitting his opinions for all to hear.

Eager to be anywhere else, using Heath as an excuse worked like a charm. Mr. Pierce patted her arm, gave her a piece of Juicy Fruit and told her to have a good day. Thank goodness.

Fifteen minutes later, Heath, clunking along in Tommy Ringwald's loaner truck, picked her up outside the salon. He popped out of the truck, limped around the front and opened the passenger door, waiting for her to get in.

"You sure you want to ride with me?" he asked, expression slightly amused.

No one had opened her door since her wedding day. She was kind of flattered. "You're not going to run off in another ditch, are you?"

"Not today." He flashed a dangerous grin and slammed the door. Cassie's stomach jumped and the reaction didn't have a thing to do with the metallic sound of a rusty old door.

Perplexed, she adjusted her skirt, tugging the red hem to her knees while Heath circled the front of the truck. He was still limping and she couldn't help thinking the injury was worse than he'd said. She also thought he looked good in navy slacks and a light blue polo. Really good. Fit, trim. Nice.

Oh, that troublesome stomach. She needed a Tums.

Heath slid onto the bench seat and started the truck. The movement whipped the spring air and released the slightly oily scent of Tommy's mechanic bay and Heath's dark woodsy aftershave. The combination was heady and manly and a huge change from the usual froufrou scents at the beauty salon.

"Did you see Dr. Ron this week?" she asked.

"I did. He said I'm fit as a fiddle and should stop slacking before the town council fires me."

"You lie." She softened the phrase with a slight smile.

"And you smell good, so we're even." He put the truck in gear and headed out of town.

She sniffed her wrist. Funny how all she could smell was him. "Distracters don't work with me. I have a brother. What did Dr. Ron really say?"

"You're a hard woman."

"Dr. Ron said that about me?"

And then they both laughed.

Heath drove like a man who'd spent plenty of time behind the wheel. Relaxed but focused, one wrist loosely draped over the steering wheel while holding the bottom with the opposite hand. He wore the watch she remembered from the accident. The glow-in-the-dark military piece.

"I'd put in a CD but this truck doesn't have a player," he said.

"Too bad. I guess you'll have to sing. What?" she asked when he looked appalled. "Don't you want to keep me entertained on this long, boring trip?"

"I want you to survive this long, boring trip."

"Okay, then, I guess you'll have to talk."

So they did and the trip wasn't long or boring at all.

Cassie Blackwell missed her calling. She should have gone into interrogations. Except Heath didn't exactly feel interrogated. He felt relaxed and he'd laughed more today in their journey from dealership to dealership than he had since the last time he'd been home with the family. She was witty and sharp and kept him on his toes. Interesting, too, with very astute input on car buying.

Now, after an entertaining lunch at Olive Garden in which Cassie had shared a crazy story about climbing behind the waterfall to pray, he had narrowed his vehicle choices to two SUVs. Same make and model, different colors and options.

"This one is really nice, Heath." Cassie drew in a deep breath as she rubbed her hand over the tan leather seats. "I love the smell of new cars."

He liked it, too. Buttery soft leather was a no brainer. Since he'd been old enough to pay his own way, all his vehicles had contained leather seats. Now, he went for the luxury. Heated and cooled seats, memory positions—not that anyone else was going to be driving his truck. Pricey but worth it.

"What do you think? Red or black? Both are loaded with all the options I want." They had just returned from a second test drive of the sparkling new black SUV. Cassie sat in the passenger seat, checking out all the options while the salesman rode along in back.

"If you're driving it for work, the red will stand out more."

"Which could be a bad thing."

"Spoken like a sneaky cop."

"I think I'll go with the black." He spoke to the salesman that hung on to every word like a hungry puppy. Scratch that. Like a hungry shark. "Knock off seven grand and include title and tax and you've got a deal."

The salesman—Jack—looked pained. "I could go three, but seven…"

"Five." Heath clapped him on the shoulder. "Come on, Jack. Cut me a deal. The lady's tired of looking." He didn't know if that was true or not. Fact was, she was perky as ever, and he wasn't all that fired up to end their day. He was, however, tired of bartering with salesmen.

Jack scribbled frantically on a notepad. Finally, he looked up. "I think we can do that. Come on inside the office and we'll start the paperwork."

Heath shot Cassie a triumphant wink. She gave him a thumbs-up and a sassy grin. Yes, sir, today was going his way.

With Cassie's high heels clicking on the concrete lot and his blood pumping with excitement over the new set of wheels, Heath followed the salesman inside the showroom and into a small office.

They were halfway through the paperwork, slowed by an enthusiastic conversation between the salesman and Cassie about whether men should color their hair or not, when Heath's cell phone vibrated.

He glanced at the number. "I better get this. It's Chief Farnsworth. Will you excuse me a minute?"

He rose from the plush chair. Police business shouldn't be discussed in public and he could think of no other reason why the chief would be calling. "I'll take this outside."

"Go ahead." Cassie waved him away with a smile that settled over him warm and sweet. Barely focused on the call, he said hello and walked out under the awning.

"You about done lollygagging in Fayetteville?" Chief Farnsworth asked with her usual bluster and without a word of greeting.

He turned his back on the showroom window and the distraction inside to stare out over a sea of shining new cars and trucks. Traffic zipped past on the four-lane running in front of the dealership.

"Finishing up the paperwork now. What's going on?"

"Ran into some information I thought might interest you."

"About?"

"The reports came back on the packaging we found. Cocaine, all right. I'm thinking the place may have been a destination for smuggled cocaine and a cooking house for crack which would end up on the streets of Arkansas."

"Figures. Anything on Louis Carmichael?"

"Yep. Nice rap sheet. Mostly piddly misdemeanors but he's been on the radar since he was a teenager."

"Any leads on where he is now?"

"No. Disappeared like smoke, but he'll turn up. Bad eggs always do." She cleared her throat. "Heard something else of interest too when I was poking around. Don't know if it's connected or a case of bad timing, but his cousin, a fella name of Darrell Chapman, may have stayed there for a short time. And now he's dead."

Heath wrinkled his forehead in thought. Where had he heard that name? The concussion no longer banged like a ten-year-old drummer, but Heath was still muzzy on some things. "Darrell Chapman? The name sounds vaguely familiar."

"It might. You had lunch with his widow the other day."

"Cassie?"

Heath spun to gaze through the showroom window at the black-haired woman chatting away with the car salesman. A knot thickened in his throat.

Was sweet, friendly, *attractive* Cassie Blackwell involved in drug trafficking?

Chapter Six

For Cassie, the day with Heath had been a blast and if she received more than usual amount of teasing at the salon afterward, she didn't care. She was into friendships, not romance. Take the mayor, for instance. Good friend. They had dinner often, went to events together, but they were nothing but friends. Same with every man before and since Darrell. Friendships lasted longer than romance. And in her case, even marriage.

Driving home in the new SUV, with Heath tailing along in Tommy's clunker, had been fun, as well. She'd never felt as swanky as she had in that fancy new vehicle with all the bells and whistles. They'd had a great day together. So, Cassie was not the least bit surprised when Heath arrived on her doorstep the next evening.

"Hey," she'd said when she opened the door.

"Hi. Am I intruding?"

"Of course not. Come in."

"Sorry I didn't call first."

"Friends are welcome anytime. We aren't formal."

He stepped inside the living room where Annalisa and Austin sat cozied up on the couch, going through a baby name book for the umpteenth time. When they spotted

Heath, Austin and Annalisa exchanged speculative glances. Cassie wanted to thump their love-struck heads.

After he'd exchanged greetings with the others, Heath turned to Cassie and said, "Mind if we take a walk? I'd like to talk to you about something."

"Let me change my shoes." She hurried into the bedroom and put on sneakers, curious to know what he wanted to discuss. Was he going to ask her out? Her goofy stomach fluttered at the thought, and she didn't understand why. Heath was her friend. Like Mayor Fairchild, they could hang out together. No big deal. But the more she thought about the upcoming conversation, the more nervous her belly.

From the living room, she heard the rumble of male voices as the men talked weather and Heath's new vehicle. When she returned, the living room was empty. She looked outside to see her brother with his head under the hood of Heath's sparkling new Expedition. The butterflies settled down. Heath was showing off his ride.

Laughing, she jogged out to them. "Nice wheels, huh?"

"Amazing." Bent at the waist, her brother turned his head toward Heath. "You have GPS?"

"Yep."

"Satellite radio?"

"Your sister said it was essential." He flashed her a grin. "And the engine has power like you wouldn't believe."

"Man." Austin straightened. "Towing package?"

"Yep. That, too. Want to take her for a spin?" Heath dug in his pocket and dangled the keys.

"You sure?"

"I wouldn't have offered otherwise. Go ahead. Enjoy."

"Thanks." Austin's expression was as excited as a kid on Christmas. "Come on, darlin'," he said to Annalisa. "Let's test drive this baby."

Annalisa cocked her head, a twinkle in her blue eyes. "Does this mean we're buying an SUV?"

Austin grinned and patted her tummy. "You never know. Babies need plenty of room."

"Well, since you put it that way…" Annalisa waddled toward the passenger door.

With tenderness, her brother assisted his pregnant wife into the vehicle, waved and drove away.

"That was nice of you."

Heath shrugged. "It's a guy thing. No big deal. Now, about that walk?"

The butterflies returned and brought their cousins. "Have you seen Whisper Falls yet?"

"No, but you told me about it yesterday. The place where people pray."

"Among other things." She still felt a little foolish about her own trek behind the falls. She wasn't sure why she'd done it. A person could pray anywhere, and the death-defying climb hadn't done her a bit of good. "It's a gorgeous area for picnics and swimming, hiking, too. Let's walk that direction. Even if we don't make it all the way, you'll hear the water and smell the river. These woods are beautiful."

Spring had exploded into full bloom with tiny yellow and white flowers carpeting the ground. Birds dipped from earth to tree and fence post, courting. The evening was cool, but not cold, and the sky a blue-gray with building clouds in the southwest.

"More rain tonight," Heath said.

"Probably. The ground is a little soggy in spots. Watch your step."

They crossed the backyard and walked through the pasture leading out of the small valley that cradled the ranch and up into the mountain. The grade was a long, easy incline she'd ridden or walked many times, particularly in the days after Darrell's death when she'd needed to be alone, to cry and ask the questions God never answered. She'd never understand some things in life, but she'd learned that God's love was there to guide her through any storm.

"Are those Austin's cattle?" Heath asked, pointing to a large herd of black Angus.

"Yes, and his horses, too. Except for the buttermilk-colored one. She's mine. Do you ride?"

"City boy, remember?"

"Oh, that's right. Bless your heart." And then she laughed. "Sorry, didn't mean that in a derogatory manner."

"No offense taken. I rode a pony at the fair when I was a kid. One of those that goes around in a circle. Does that count?"

"Everybody has to start somewhere." She laughed again. She had done that a lot the last two days.

They walked along in silence for a ways. Heath stopped once to pick a cluster of bright pink flowers—phlox, she thought, but wasn't sure. Her friend, Haley would know. Flowers were her passion.

"For enduring yesterday's car hunt," he said, presenting them to her.

"Nice." Cassie sniffed the small blooms. "I really didn't mind. It was actually fun." Which said so much about her social life.

"For me, too. You're good company." He wiped a hand down the leg of his jeans and looked off toward the mountains. She could see he had something on his mind and didn't know how to start, so she decided to help him.

"All right, now. Let's get down to business. What did you want to discuss? An appointment for that mani-pedi? Walk-ins are welcome at Tress and Tan."

She gave him an impish look, surprised when he didn't

respond to the tease. His sense of humor was one of the things she liked about him. "Why so serious?"

"Just wondering about some things."

"Like what?"

His eyes found hers and held. She tried to read their green depths but came up empty.

"Your marriage, for one. Chief told me your husband died on your honeymoon. I'm sorry."

The topic surprised her a little. Surprised and jabbed. She hadn't seen that one coming. She turned aside and gazed into the deep green forest. The woods seemed silent and empty but she knew they teemed with life. "Me, too, but thank you. Losing him so soon was horrible. We just didn't have enough time, but when we met, I saw forever in his eyes. It probably sounds silly and overly romantic but I knew he was the one."

"Just like that, huh? Bam! Love at first sight?"

"Exactly." She smiled a little, remembering. "He walked into the Iron Horse snack shop and ordered a Sprite and a bag of Cheetos. I was sitting at the bar talking to Uncle Digger when he noticed me and ordered another Sprite and a bag of Cheetos, sending them down to me. He grinned and raised his paper cup in a toast." She sighed. "And I was a goner."

As she'd intended, Heath chuckled. "Sprite and Cheetos are the way to a woman's heart."

"To mine anyway. There was something so easy and carefree about Darrell. I don't know how to explain love, but I adored him and he adored me. He did so many little things that made me feel loved."

"How long had you been together?"

"Four weeks and six days."

Heath stopped in his tracks. "Four weeks?"

She'd expected his shock. Her friends and family had

been even more stunned. "Darrell had only been in town a short time to visit his cousin when we met. But those few weeks was all I needed to fall in love. Austin thought I was crazy, but when he saw how happy Darrell and I were together, he gave his blessing."

"So you got married."

"Eloped. Well, sort of. We went to the courthouse in Whisper Falls and Judge Olsen married us."

"Where was the honeymoon?"

"Mexico. I'd never been, but Darrell loved Mexico and wanted to show it to me. The water is so clear you can see the fish, and the beach is glorious."

"I'll have to agree. Beautiful place."

"You've been there?"

He picked up a rock, gave it a fling. It clattered in the distance. "Cancun is spectacular. Snorkeling there is the best."

"Darrell took me snorkeling and I loved looking at the pretty fish. He preferred to scuba dive. I wasn't ready for that. He dove. I snorkeled and played on the beach."

"Is that what happened to him? An accident while diving?"

Cassie pressed her lips together. The sun had gone behind a cloud and the air was cooler. She crossed her arms against the chill. "Apparently."

"Weren't you with him?"

"I should have been." Though she'd learned not to feel guilty or responsible, she did have regret. "We'd had the best day together on the water, and Darrell wanted to go out one more time. I was tired and wanted to stay at the hotel, so he ordered room service for me and a massage. So sweet and thoughtful." She smiled sadly at the memory. "When night came and he didn't return, I knew something had happened. Darrell wouldn't have purposely worried me."

Though she was over the terrible screaming grief, that

long Mexican night and the next gorgeous sunny morning were indelibly imprinted on her memory. In a foreign country, she hadn't known where to turn. She'd contacted the hotel security who were no help at all, saying that her husband was probably drunk somewhere or having a fling. Not her Darrell, not her brand-new husband.

"When did they find him?"

"Later that afternoon. He'd washed up on a remote beach. Drowned." She shook her head. "I never understood that. He was such a great swimmer and in terrific shape."

"Do you mind if I ask what Darrell did for a living?"

She pivoted toward him, suddenly aware of a tension in his words that hadn't been there before. Suddenly wondering why Heath was asking so many questions. "Why?"

"Just wondering." He shrugged, a look that spoke of nonchalance, but Cassie had a feeling he wasn't casual at all. There was something going on here that had nothing to do with romantic interest in her or simple curiosity about her late husband.

She studied Heath's poker face for several long quiet seconds before saying, "He was in sales."

Heath's green gaze slid away from hers. He reached in his pocket with one hand. "Did he say what kind of sales?"

"Pharmaceutical. He told me before we married that he would have to travel a lot in his work. He was the sweetest man. He wanted to be sure I could handle the alone time." She kicked at a rock with the toe of her shoe. "I never got a chance to find out."

"I really am sorry, Cassie."

His sympathy defused her defensiveness. Maybe she was imagining things. Friends could ask friends about anything. Right?

"I'm okay now. He's been gone nearly three years and life goes on. Anyway, that's what my big brother tells me."

"A loss like that never goes away. The pain dulls, you move on, but you don't forget."

Of course, Heath would understand. He'd been there with his father. Knowing they shared a similar heartache made her feel close to him—in a friendship kind of way. "You were only a little boy. Losing your dad must have impacted your entire life."

"I guess you could say that." He cupped a palm beneath her elbow as they started up an incline that led toward the river.

"You should be able to hear the waterfall from atop this rise," she said. "There's the Blackberry River below. See it? Like a silver ribbon through the green trees? The water flows down from the falls and winds through this valley past the edge of town."

They stood atop a ridge with the river below and the forest to their left. Beyond was a wildness of woods and sky and stunning spring landscape, green and blooming. Dogwoods, he thought. "The view's nice from up here."

"It's glorious." She stretched her arms wide. "The word *nice* is too puny."

"I stand corrected." He gave her a lopsided smile she found charming. Even though a strange heaviness nagged in the pit of her stomach, she found a lot of things about Heath charming.

"Want to climb the rest of the way up to Whisper Falls? We still have another mile to go."

"No, this is far enough." He drew in a deep breath and looked up into the sky. The sun was starting to ease toward the western horizon, a giant orange ball against a graying sky. "Listen, Cassie, I need to ask you something important. You may not like it."

The knot in her belly tightened and grew hot. She'd been

right. There was more to Heath's questions than friendly conversation.

Though his face gave nothing away, his voice and posture were tense, watchful.

"Okaaay. You're kind of making me nervous. What is it?"

"All right, here's my question. Straight out." He thrust both hands in his pockets as if he didn't trust them. "Did you ever get the feeling Darrell wasn't what he seemed? Did you wonder if he kept secrets from you?"

"No! He wouldn't."

"Are you positive?"

Maybe a few times, but they were still in the early days of getting to know each other. "Why would you ask such a thing? What is going on, Heath? Do you know something about Darrell that I don't?"

"I'm not going to jump to conclusions. This is a fact-finding mission." His hands went deeper into his pockets. His jaw was tight and hard.

"You're investigating Darrell?" Her voice rose in agitation. Her fingers tightened on the cluster of flowers. "That's crazy. He was a wonderful man."

"Did you know his cousin, Louis?"

"We met a few times. He didn't seem to like me much. Why? What does any of this have to do with anything?"

Her knees had started to shake and she wanted to sit down. No, she wanted to run back to the house and tell Heath to take his weird questions somewhere else. What had happened to the charming, funny man of yesterday?

"Louis's trailer blew away in the tornado."

Alarm raced along her nerve endings and prickled the nape of her neck. She was becoming more confused by the minute. "Is he okay?"

"We don't know. He wasn't there. We were hoping you might know where he would go after losing his home."

"We? Heath, is this official police business?"

"Do you know Louis's whereabouts, Cassie?"

"No, I don't. When Darrell died, he seemed angry, as if I was to blame. We haven't spoken since the funeral."

"Did you know anything about Louis's business interests?"

"No." She crossed her arms over her racing heart, crushing the scent from the tiny blooms. "Heath, I don't understand all these questions. What's going on? Please, I thought we were friends. Tell me what this is about."

"We *are* friends, Cassie, and I owe you. I don't like asking all these questions, but they're important and you're the only lead I have." He stepped toward her, the sun gilding his dark hair, and tugged at her arms. "We have reason to believe Louis may have been involved in the drug trade."

"No," she breathed.

"Did you ever see or hear anything that made you suspicious?"

She shook her head. "I went to his trailer with Darrell only once and it was so junky and cluttered, I didn't want to be there. Louis didn't want me there, either. He was upset with Darrell for some reason and they went off by themselves to talk. When we left, Darrell was in a bad mood."

"Could Darrell have been working with Louis?"

"Absolutely not!" she said hotly.

"Okay, okay." Heath raised both hands in surrender. "No more questions. You're killing that poor flower."

Cassie uncrossed her arms and stared at the pink phlox. She felt as wadded and bruised as it looked. "Darrell was a good man, Heath."

"I hope so, Cassie." Heath's warm hand closed over hers. "For your sake, I hope so."

Chapter Seven

All night and into the next morning, Heath's brain whirled with the information he'd gotten from Cassie. He didn't want to believe she was involved in anything illicit, but she wouldn't be the first good citizen who'd gotten caught up in the money generated by the illegal-drug industry. Yet he couldn't just toss away the fact that she'd been there for him when he'd needed someone. Not once, but twice. And he liked her. A lot.

He also knew the danger of getting emotionally involved during an investigation, especially with his only lead. The job came first. Dad deserved that much from him, regardless of his interest in a pretty woman. There were plenty of pretty women. He had only one dad.

Ruminating his next move in the investigation, he drove the gleaming black Expedition up and down the streets of Whisper Falls, stopping now and then to talk or to investigate the out-of-ordinary. Folks were friendly and interested in the new vehicle and the new police officer. Good folks, mostly, though he knew from experience even the most peaceful towns harbored a dark element. He'd come to Whisper Falls in need of that peace and quiet and already he'd encountered the darkness.

He should have expected as much. Ferreting out darkness seemed to be his calling.

Removing Dad's badge from his pocket, he placed it on the dash where he could see it. His father had taught him to seek the truth because the truth would set him free. Today he felt as if seeking the truth bound him tighter than any ropes or chains ever could.

Cassie was involved, one way or the other. The question was how did he find out which?

He stopped at the courthouse to meet with the chief. As he entered the side door, he greeted Verletta, the day-shift dispatcher who handed him the thick stack of today's mail. At fifty-something, Verletta wore her blond hair to her shoulders and a pair of red plastic glasses perched on her nose. She knew the job and the town and everybody's ancestry clear back to the war of aggression and thought nothing of calling up Heath or the chief, for that matter, with the message, "You'd better get on down there." She made him smile but he always went because, for all her unorthodox methods and raspy-voiced commands, Verletta was rarely wrong. As usual, this morning she had a fountain Coke the size of a pitcher within easy reach—to keep the whistle clear, as she put it.

Mail tucked under his arm, Heath went on through to the chief's office and found her rummaging through a file drawer as if she wanted to rip someone's head off. He hoped it wasn't his. He tossed the packet of mail on her desk and said, "You look annoyed."

"I *am* annoyed. Been up since three this morning. Didn't Verletta tell you? A couple of idiots busted into one of the senior units."

Heath tensed. "Why didn't you call me?"

"You're still recovering. I handled it."

"I'm recovered. Stop coddling me." He fisted his hands

on his hips, as annoyed as she looked. "Did you catch the perps?"

"Caught them, wanted to knock their heads, but turned them over to the parents. That's why I'm mad. Those kids have been in trouble before and their parents always make excuses and bail them out."

"A night in jail might scare some better behavior into them."

"My thoughts, too, but being juveniles the law is lenient."

"They won't be juvies forever. The seniors all right?"

"Scared. Shaken. Mr. Abernathy had a heart spell which meant Dr. Ron had an early-morning call, too. He'll be all right." She barked her laugh. "Both of them."

"Anything else I need to know about?"

"Check the log. Anytime there's a break-in, the elders get spooked and we get calls." She slammed the file cabinet. The sound ricocheted off the walls.

Heath had a feeling the chief was wishing she could slam some heads instead of metal drawers. He understood. He'd been there, but a good cop did his job and left the rest to the courts, as hard as that often was. "I'll spend some extra time at the complex today. Park the truck, walk around, say hello."

"Good plan. Knock on a few doors and introduce yourself. Make them feel safe again." She tossed a manila folder onto her desk. "Could Cassie Blackwell shine any light on the Carmichael investigation?"

"How did you know I talked to Cassie?"

"Had coffee at the Iron Horse. Annalisa told Digger who told me that you and Cassie took a long, romantic walk."

Small town grapevine. Heath snorted. "Any idea how long Darrell Chapman was in the area before he and Cassie hooked up?"

"Not really, but it bears checking. Don't know when he came to visit his cousin, either, but he hadn't been around long. If he was, he stayed in the woods. You're thinking the deceased was involved?"

"Maybe. Probably. Either that or he showed up innocently and learned something that got him killed."

The chief's eyebrows went up. "His death was ruled an accident."

"Yeah. In Mexico where it's simpler and cleaner to say a tourist had an accident."

"You're the expert." Heath could see the wheels turning in a very sharp, if somewhat eccentric mind. All cops were a different breed. Some were just more different than others. "What do you think happened down in Mexico?"

"I'm mulling a few theories." And didn't like any of them. "How long have you known Cassie?"

The roller chair clattered on the tile as Chief Farnsworth yanked it back from the desk to settle in. "She moved here with her brother, Austin, about six or seven years ago, as I recollect."

"So, how well do you know her?"

The chief began to rifle through the mail, tossing unopened junk in the too-full trash can. Did she ever empty that thing?

"Her granddaddy owned the piece of property where the ranch is now. I knew him. Good people. I have a hard time believing James Blackwell's granddaughter is involved with drug dealers, if that's what you're getting at. If her husband was running drugs, she may not have known."

"Maybe. But we have a job to find out."

"Suspicious sort, aren't you?"

"Pretty much." Came with the territory.

The chief paused from the wild sorting event to laser him with a long, intent look. "Word of caution, Monroe.

Cassie is well-liked in this town. I wouldn't let word get around that you think she's involved in drug trafficking unless you have some very solid evidence. In the meantime, step lightly."

"I plan to." He believed in the scripture: "wise as serpents and gentle as doves." At least the wise part. He was working on the gentle. "Why don't you take a breather, get some rest. My leg's good today. I can handle the rest of the shift while you catch up on sleep from last night."

"Don't put me out to pasture, Monroe. Between me and the handful of part-timers, I've been policing this town nearly as long as you've been alive." She tossed him an envelope. "Take your paycheck and get busy earning the next one."

Pulling to the curb outside the bank, Heath's gaze drifted down the street to the Tress and Tan. A mature woman, snazzily dressed and carrying a bright yellow handbag, entered the building. He wondered if she was there to see Cassie.

Inside the bank, he handed over his first official paycheck for deposit into his brand-new account. While he waited for the receipt and some petty cash for his wallet, he leaned an elbow on the slick counter and scoped out the space. Did JoEtta have a blueprint of the bank on file in case of robbery? As the chief claimed, he was a suspicious sort, seeing crime before it happened.

Two other tellers were busy with customers, a farmer in overalls, a young mother with a toddler hanging on to her leg. A scattering of desks was inhabited by equally busy employees typing away on computers or rummaging through paperwork. Through the glass-enclosed offices, he located the bank officials, including Michelle Jessup. His gaze lingered for a moment longer than he'd intended. The blonde was elegant and high-end in a straight mustard-colored dress and black jacket with pearls at her throat, wrist and ears. She must have felt his stare because she glanced up. Immediately, she rose from her desk and came out to greet him.

"Why, Heath, what a nice start to the morning. How is that awful leg injury?" She was much lower key here in the bank than she'd been in the salon. More professional friendly than over-the-top flirtatious. He kind of liked the change.

"Healing. Thanks." As soon as he said it, his ankle shot pain up to his knee just to spite him.

"What brings you in this morning? A loan for that gorgeous new SUV?"

"I have that covered already, but I appreciate the offer." A man whose lifestyle was too busy to spend much money and who'd had an expense account for the rest could save a lot over the years.

"Well, shoot. I could have fixed you up."

He imagined she could have. "Maybe next time."

Michelle beamed at him with a bright, beautiful smile that probably cost more than he'd made in his first year of work. Someone had told him, Verletta he thought, that Michelle was the only child of the pharmacist and the only granddaughter of a well-to-do family. She was accustomed to money and attention.

"If you have a few minutes, come on in my office for coffee. We'll talk. I want to be sure our bank is treating you well." She winked. "Don't want to lose you."

The teller returned at the moment to count out his change. Turning slightly, not wanting to be rude to either woman, Heath stuck his hand out toward the teller.

"Can't today. I'm on duty."

Behind him, the teller counted out his cash. He only half

listened because Michelle's long-fingered hand touched his elbow. "Rain check?"

Why not? He was new in town. She was attractive and they were both available, although he had a feeling she might be more available than he was. Still, she was interested, and he had nothing to go home to but a big-screen television and his own thoughts. "A rain check sounds good."

As he walked out into the overcast day, he sent another look toward the Tress and Tan, a reminder of the investigation he'd only begun. Michelle might be a pleasant distraction but Cassie needed to be his focus. He didn't like having to play her, but an agent did what he had to do. If Cassie was involved in a trafficking scheme, the subterfuge would be worth the effort. He wondered what she was doing for lunch….

Cassie sat across the table from Heath, still questioning why she'd agreed to this last-minute lunch invitation. She wanted to be angry with him after last night. He'd accused Darrell, the sweetest man ever, of being a criminal. But that was impossible, and she wanted to make Heath understand as much. The length of time she'd known Darrell didn't matter. He'd adored her. He had treated her like a queen, like a gorgeous woman instead of a buddy who gave free haircuts.

"What do you recommend?" Heath asked, tapping the menu with a knuckle. "I've never eaten here before."

"Everything tastes good. Home cooked and fresh. I like the cheeseburger and cottage fries but I'm a junk food lover."

"Kindred spirits, then. A cheeseburger sounds good."

Kindred spirits? She didn't think so, though she had to admit she'd liked him until last night. Today, he was cool as a cucumber mask, behaving as if he hadn't insulted her late husband's memory, as if they were the best of friends. Strange, confusing man.

"You're quiet today." He pushed the one sheet, plastic-covered menu to the end of the table.

"I don't hear that very often." She held his gaze, not smiling, laced fingers in a death grip. It was unusual for Cassie not to smile at everyone, but today Heath was a bug under inspection. Until he got off Darrell's back, he was on her bad side. A people person, she didn't often have one of those, but Heath Monroe had found it.

He must have read her tension because he leaned forward and placed a hand atop her clasped ones—and surprised the daylights out of her. They were less than a yard apart. Mere inches, really. Completely disconcerting.

Cassie could see a razor nick beneath Heath's soul patch, a little swatch of whiskers beneath his bottom lip. Very faint lines had begun to form across his forehead and around his eyes. All together, they gave him a slight bad-boy look.

"Mad at me?"

"A little," she admitted, though if she was *really* mad, she should move her hands from beneath his warm, strong grasp and stop staring at his mouth and eyes. She was mad. She really was. But she didn't move.

"I'm sorry if I upset you. I didn't want to. Forgive me?"

Well, since he put it that way. To withhold forgiveness was wrong. "If you won't talk about Darrell anymore."

Very green eyes—eyes as dark and mysterious as jade—rested on her face. Sitting this close to a man who held both her hands and her gaze with a burning intensity should have felt threatening, or at the least uncomfortable. Instead, her breath grew a little shorter and her toes tingled.

The waiter chose that opportune moment to return with their order. Flustered at being seen holding hands with the new assistant police chief, a man she didn't want to like, Cassie jerked her hands away. Heath sat back against the red vinyl booth, a soft, quizzical expression on his face.

What in the world had just happened? Her neck was hot. Her pulsed raced as if an electric current ran from him straight into her heart. She sat back, too, and took a deep breath, filling her lungs with fresh-food smells instead of Heath Monroe. Cassie Blackwell did not get flustered over a man. Ever. Time to get this lunch back on her terms.

"To friends," she said, lifting her burger after the waiter had left.

He raised his sandwich in a toast. "Friends sounds good."

Cassie bit into the juicy hamburger, mollified by his easy manner. Whatever had sparked in her had obviously not affected Heath. Which was good, right?

"How's the ankle?"

"Practically healed. Only aches if I'm up too long. The doc cut me loose." He took a sip of Coke, grabbed a fry. "So, fill me in on all the gossip. What do the experts at Tress and Tan say is going on in Whisper Falls that a peace officer should know about?"

"Jed Thompson and Marty Bates broke into the Abernathys' apartment this morning. That's the big news of the day. The little twerps."

He titled his sandwich toward her. "Already know about that one."

"Oh, I guess you would. I hope they get in big trouble for scaring Mr. Abernathy like that. Karen Littlejohn—she works at the Quick Stop on the corner by the senior complex—said Doctor Ron was called out and all the seniors were scared and upset."

"They are. I spent some time with them this morning, did a walk-through of the yards, even went inside if they asked me. Met Creed Carter's granny. Nice lady but I think she could hold her own against a burglar with that cane of hers."

"Did she share her peanut candy?"

"How did you know?"

"That's Granny Carter. She'll make you some biscuits and gravy, too, if you hang around long enough."

"Do I hear the voice of experience?"

"Mmm-hmm," she said as she finished chewing a bite and swallowed. "I'm sure the residents feel better for having you check things out. It was thoughtful of you."

"Just doing my job."

She didn't care if it was his duty. Taking time to ease worries was a good thing to do and she liked him better for it. "Did you hear that Miss Evelyn and the city council set this Saturday as community spring cleaning?"

"Missed that. Tell me about it."

So she did, and as she talked and ate, two things guaranteed to relax her, the tension left her shoulders. Never one to hold a grudge, Cassie enjoyed people too much to remain angry. She knew Darrell was not a criminal, and that was all that mattered.

"Can you do me a favor?"

Inside his apartment that evening, Heath flopped onto his couch, cell phone to his ear, talking to his brother in Houston.

"What now?" Holt asked in a wry voice. "You need money?"

Heath snorted. "Doesn't everybody? You want to give me a million or two?"

"The check's in the mail, like always." Holt chuckled at the familiar joke. "What's up?"

Heath propped one hand behind his head and pictured his younger brother. Taller than Heath at six-three, and rangy like a major-league pitcher, the dark-haired, dark-eyed Holt was a martial arts black belt who could take a man down faster than a bullet. Heath should know. He'd been the guinea pig too many times. Holt looked like everybody's best friend, but beneath the amiable smile was one tough PI.

"Family first. How are Krissy and the kids?"

"Good. Ashley's had a cold and is a grump."

Heath's heart squeezed. Ashley was his four-year-old niece. He'd walk on fire for that dimpled darling. For all of them if push came to shove.

"Give her a hug from Uncle Heath and tell her I love her. The boys, too."

"Will do. Now what's this favor you want?"

"I need you to take a trip to Mexico."

"Mexico? Why do I have a feeling this isn't a vacation?"

"You could make it one. Take Krissy and the kids."

"Am I paying for this little getaway?"

"If it's a vacation you are."

"No vacation then. Spill. What's in Mexico?"

"I'm not sure anything is but I'm working an investigation into possible drug trafficking out of there."

Holt whistled softly. "Bad place for that, son. *Bad* place."

"Don't I know it?" He'd been up to his eyeballs in trouble in Mexico more than once.

"So here's the deal. Whisper Falls had a tornado the night I came in."

"I remember. Ran you off in a ditch. How's the bum ankle?"

"Good." He'd downplayed the accident for the sake of his mother, not wanting her to feel the need to fly to Arkansas. All Holt knew about was a sprained ankle. It wasn't the first time he'd kept an injury to himself. "After the storm, someone reported damage in the rural areas. That's when we stumbled onto a demolished trailer, paraphernalia and a missing home owner."

"In Whisper Falls? The rural town you described as a quiet little place in the mountains where you could chill for a while?"

"It is. But you know me and drugs. We have this ongoing war. If they're around, I find them." Or maybe they found him. Either way, the battle raged.

"Still carrying Dad's badge?"

"Always."

There was a hum of quiet between the brothers that filled in the gaps. No words were needed. They both knew why Heath did what he did. Their father was the reason all of them were in law enforcement.

Finally, Holt broke the silence. "What's the connection with Mexico?"

"The evidence reeks of Mexican cartel. Cocaine. Probably smuggled up from Colombia and repackaged for the U.S. Add to that the troubling issue of a man who lived or stayed briefly in that house. Name of Darrell Chapman. He and his new bride honeymooned in Mexico and he turns up dead on a pretty Mexican beach."

Holt made a low noise in the back of his throat. "I'm starting to smell something."

"Yeah, something stinks, all right. But other than the evidence found in the trailer, all of this is circumstantial. The man could have been an innocent bystander with no knowledge of his cousin's side business. And he could have very well drowned as the death certificate claims."

"Or the honeymoon could have been a setup, a meeting place, a drop-off or pickup. Then our Darrell boy could have made someone unhappy and gotten himself whacked."

"That's what I need to know. Will you check it out for me?" Heath thought of his lunch with Cassie and his conscience twinged a little but the job came first. For her sake he hoped Darrell was clean as Ozark spring water.

"Why not turn the case over to your pals at the DEA and let them handle it?"

"I can't. Not yet. It's personal." His own words caught Heath by surprise.

Holt held on through a beat of awareness. "A woman?"

"Maybe," he admitted as much to himself as to his brother. If Darrell was dirty he wanted justice done, but he didn't want Cassie hurt in the process. He wasn't sure why she was any more important than any other case he'd been involved with, but she was.

"Don't tell me it's the widow."

"All right, I won't. Got a pencil? I'll give you the details."

"Who said I was going?"

Heath just laughed.

Chapter Eight

Heath's suspicions had bugged her for days. Even though the new assistant chief had kept his word and said nothing more about Darrell, the question of her husband's innocence hung between them on every occasion. And there had been a lot of those since the hamburger outing.

As if he was trying to make up for the wound he'd inflicted, Heath turned up frequently to take her to lunch, to help with the storm clean-up, and last night he'd even stopped by at closing time with a pizza.

Figuratively speaking, a girl could fall in love with a man who enjoyed a thick crust supreme with double cheese and Canadian bacon as much as she did. Though the ladies at the salon tried to fan the flames of romance, Cassie simply rolled her eyes and carried on. Given her track record with men, they should know a friendship when they spotted one. Darrell was her one and only, but being nice to the new people in town came naturally. It was who she was—even if the newcomer was especially handsome and charming and male.

Still, Cassie was strangely disquieted that she could like Heath at all. That she could get an extra buzz of energy when he cruised past in his big, fancy Expedition or popped into the shop to say hello. And that on this Saturday evening after a long day on her feet, she would be eager to leave the relaxed comfort of her PJs and crochet hook. But she was.

"You look amazing." Annalisa waddled in from her evening walk, moving slower by the day. Her newly full face glowed with the effort. One hand rubbed round and round on her large belly; Tootsie, the apricot poodle, trotted alongside, a willing but unlikely protector.

"Thank you." Cassie glanced down at her attire. Nothing fancy. Jeans and bright blue top with strappy heels. The usual. Except for the chiffon scarf and blingy bracelet she'd added. And the spritz of perfume. "You look miserable tonight."

Annalisa groaned as she stretched her back. "I feel miserable, too. Junior here is taking up space I don't have."

"A few more weeks and you can breathe again."

"Yes, thank the good Lord." With affection and pride, the pretty blonde patted the top of her belly. "Is Heath coming over?"

"Should be here any minute. We're going to the concert in the park. He's unofficially on duty, as always, and needed a friend to hang out with."

Her sister-in-law smiled a Mona Lisa smile that suggested more than friendship was in the air.

"Don't start," Cassie said, pointing a freshly done nail. "I get enough grief at the salon."

"Then why not admit you like him for more than a friend?"

"Friendship is all I have to offer."

"Love can come more than once in a lifetime, sweetie."

"Not for me." She'd been numb so long she wouldn't know love if it dyed its hair chartreuse and rode shotgun in her Nissan.

"He's a terrific guy. Everyone seems to like him and he

goes to church, too." Annalisa pointed a puffy finger. "You should give him a chance."

Cassie had never told either Austin or Annalisa about Heath's insinuations, of how he'd insulted Darrell's good name. She didn't want anyone to think less of her late husband and a stain on his reputation was sure to happen if word got around. The sting had faded but she hadn't forgotten what Heath had done. She couldn't. "Friends, Annalisa. That's all."

Her sister-in-law eased her swollen body into a chair, holding the padded arm as she went down with a groaning sigh. "Look at the size of my feet!"

"Whoa, honey! You have to get those puppies elevated."

At the word *puppies,* Tootsie trotted to her side and looked up with bright, eager eyes.

"Not you, darling." Cassie smooched at the dog as she pushed the ottoman into place and gently lifted Annalisa's feet. "Is your blood pressure up again?"

"A little."

Cassie gnawed the side of her cheek. From working with women all day, she knew high blood pressure could spell danger during pregnancy. "Have you called your doctor?"

"Yes, Mommy. This morning."

"Let me nag. That's my one and only nephew you have in there. Can I get you anything?"

"No, but you're sweet to offer. Austin will be in soon and he will rub my back. It's killing me today for some reason." To prove the point, she arched and squirmed trying to get comfortable. "Your brother gives the best back rubs."

A mix of sympathy and envy stirred in Cassie. As much as she delighted in her brother's happiness and the coming child, they were a constant reminder of what she had missed.

Even though Annalisa had asked for nothing, Cassie

went into the kitchen, poured a glass of filtered water and carried it to her sister-in-law. Tootsie trotted merrily along, tags jingling.

Life had certainly changed since her brother had married. The once-quiet ranch was lively with family preparations, baby talk, dreams and plans for the future. There had never been any question about her continuing to live at the ranch after their wedding, no hint that she was in the way, but sometimes she wondered. Newlyweds with a baby on the way needed their space.

But where would she go? This was home.

She went to the window, uncharacteristically discontent. A shiny black SUV wound down the long driveway.

"There's Heath," she said. "I have to grab my purse."

"He better not expect me to get out of this chair."

With a snicker, Cassie whipped her phone from her back pocket. "I'll text him a pregnant woman alert."

Annalisa's hands rested on her belly. "You do that."

Cassie hurried down the hall, grabbed her purse and the file folder she'd prepared. By the time she reached the front porch, Heath was out of his vehicle and halfway to the house. The limp that had slowed him down for weeks had disappeared, replaced by a confident stride. No swagger, no over-the-top machismo. Just confidence and strength. No wonder he was a great cop and the folks of Whisper Falls had taken him in like a native. He had an air about him that made people feel safe and protected.

"I got your text. Is everything all right with Annalisa?" he asked as they met on the grassy lawn.

"She's been like this for a week. Being nearly eight months pregnant is wearing her down." When he took her elbow, she let him guide her to the passenger side of the truck, enjoying the mannerly attention of a non-related male.

"Up you go. You look really nice."

"So do you. Green is your color." The Kelly-green shirt turned his eyes to emeralds.

"I'll blend into the grass in the park. Do-wrongs won't see me coming."

"About the only do-wrongs you'll find at a May concert in the Whisper Falls park will be teenagers making out behind the trees."

He pumped his eyebrows, his gaze dropping to her mouth. "We may have to do a stakeout."

Cassie was certain her face turned as red as her lips. The idea of kissing Heath, of the feel of his scant mustache against her mouth exploded in her head. Unable to shake the thought, she did the only thing she could. She rolled her eyes. Heath laughed. There was something about that short, intense laugh of his that sent pinpricks of pleasure dancing over her skin.

The laugh. The man. The thought of kissing him. What was wrong with her?

She tightened her grip on the file folder.

Heath saw the movement and hitched his chin toward her lap. "Whatcha got there? Words to *Rocky Top* so we can sing along?"

Cassie opened the file, letting his joke slide. Any self-respecting fan knew the words to the famous bluegrass song.

Might as well get this over with. "This is a file on Darrell."

He jerked, spun his focus toward her, eyes wide and surprised. "You kept a file on your husband?"

"No, silly. I made one." She tapped the folder. "This has our honeymoon itinerary, phone records, hotel reservations, even the bill for the flowers he sent me the day of his death.

Every record I could find or print off the computer. After you accused him of being a criminal—"

"I didn't accuse him, Cassie. Asking questions is not an accusation."

Why didn't that make her feel any better? "Then let's say you insinuated. Whatever term you want to use, you raised questions that I want answered."

"I thought you didn't want to discuss this again."

"I didn't at first but the more I think about what you said, the more it bothers me. Darrell was not a criminal. I want to help you prove that."

Heath refocused on the country lane. His square jaw worked. Nostrils flared. Finally, he gave her a quick, hard glance and said, "What if you're wrong?"

She'd thought about that, had lain awake more than one night pondering her late husband's activities, wondering if she'd been the biggest fool on earth. The questions nagged at her like an ingrown toenail, cutting into every good memory she'd treasured up to this point. Closure had become a necessity. "Louis may have been involved in bad things. That wouldn't surprise me at all. I can't believe it of Darrell."

"All right. Tell you what. If I can prove him innocent, I will. But I'll need your cooperation. Everything you know."

"These records are all I have. What else can I do?"

"Witnesses often don't know what they know. You see or hear something, some anomaly that doesn't quite fit but you blow it off thinking it's nothing."

"I guess that's possible," she said doubtfully.

"Oh, it's possible. Even likely. Trust me on that."

What choice did she have? She'd already betrayed Darrell by digging through his computer files with a suspicious eye.

"Tell me everything you know, every detail you remember, especially about the trip to Mexico."

"I did that already."

"You gave me the short version. I want the long one. Times when you weren't with Darrell. Where did he go? Who did he meet and do business with? How did he act before and after? Did anything seem out of place? Were you ever worried or suspicious? Did he ever say anything, get a strange phone call, a note he didn't let you see, anything that didn't fit?"

Cassie's gut clenched into a knot. Now she understood how people felt during an interrogation. It wasn't fun.

"Nothing."

"If you think of anything, write it down, text me, call me." Heath hammered away with rapid-fire questions, asking things she'd never considered. Cassie dug deep, searching for any clue, though nothing she told him seemed that important.

By the time she reached the park, Cassie was no longer excited about a bluegrass concert.

Heath felt like a jerk even though he shouldn't have. Extracting this kind of information from Cassie had been his intent from the start, his reason for making excuses to see her every day. Now he wasn't so sure. Part of him wanted to forget the investigation and have a good time with a woman he liked. Yet the badge in his pocket burned with the flame of justice.

The Whisper Falls Municipal Park sat at the west end of town where Easy Street became the highway leading out of town. To park, a car simply pulled off the road and found a spot. Sometimes that spot happened to be in someone's yard but as long as there was no Keep Off sign, people parked where they wanted to. It was a system that had served since the town's founding and unless progress paid for paved parking, the system would continue.

Heath found an empty, grassy space next to the funeral home—which was kitty-cornered from the park—and pulled in. He killed the vehicle and turned toward his date. A relationship that had begun as a means of obtaining information had become more. He wasn't ready to put a name to his feelings, but Cassie meant something.

"Have I put a damper on the evening with my questions?" he asked softly.

"It doesn't matter."

"Sure it does." He gently took the folder from her and slid it under the front seat. From the bandstand, a fiddle played high and sweet. "Let's put this away, try to forget about the case for a while and enjoy ourselves. The music is calling."

"Okay." But she looked so serious now.

"Hey." He tilted her chin with his thumb and stared into a pair of sorrowful irises of pale green that stayed in his mind even when he wasn't with her. Like the rest of her. Cajoling, he said, "I'll buy you a pizza. Extra large."

A hint of amusement flickered. "All to myself?"

He stroked his knuckle along her jawbone. Her alabaster skin, beautiful with her very black hair, was every bit as soft as he'd expected. Like sun-warmed rose petals. Without knowing it, he'd let her creep into his subconscious. "Only if you want to see an officer of the law salivate in public."

Her nostrils flared, the makings of a laugh, and he knew he'd won when her red lips bowed. "When do we get this pizza?"

Heath took his hand away. Brushing Cassie's skin interfered with his reasoning—and a lawman had to be alert. "Whenever you say."

"Pizza Pan stays open until midnight on Saturday night."

His mouth curved. "Concert first. Pizza later?"

"You're on, big boy." She raised her hand for a high five. He slapped her smaller palm and gave her hand a quick squeeze. A secret promise that he'd do his best to protect her, all the while hoping he didn't have to break her heart in the process.

They exited the SUV and sauntered across the freshly mowed grass into the park. Popcorn scented the air. The band was in full throttle, banjoes dueling while a stand-up bass thumped out a rhythm. Hard to stay in a dark mood with that kind of energy vibrating the airwaves.

Heath gazed around, scoping out the environment. "Good crowd."

"The weather is perfect, and Whisper Falls is known for good bluegrass events."

He catalogued the spots he considered problem areas, though he was here only as backup in case something hinky went down. No one expected that in Whisper Falls. Except him. He always expected trouble. Maybe that's why it found him so often.

The band kicked into the next number. A lively, sawing fiddle took center stage.

"Name that tune," he said.

"'Orange Blossom Special.'"

"Impressive. Are you a fan?"

She smiled. "I've been to these concerts before."

"Cheater." He snagged her hand and when she didn't pull away led them through the milling crowd. Cassie was a people magnet and stopped frequently to greet customers and friends and church members, drawing him in. For a man who'd been rootless since college, belonging to a town was different but nice. He liked the town, enjoyed the friendly Southern people.

All during the exchanges, Heath remained alert in his

role as security. When a pair of teenagers hooked up in a fight, he left Cassie with friends and hurried toward the rumble. The small circle of onlookers saw him coming and the fighters broke apart, breathing heavily. One kid had a nosebleed.

Heath stepped between them. In a calm, firm voice, he settled the issue, took the nosebleed to a makeshift first aid station and contacted parents. By the time he'd taken care of business, Cassie wasn't where he'd left her. He pulled out his cell phone and flipped through the contacts for her name. Before he could complete the call, the blonde and beautiful Michelle Jessup approached him.

"I saw what you did, Heath. So brave."

He fought an eye roll. "They're just kids."

"Still, kids today…" She shook her long hair as if she thought all of today's teenagers were one step away from mass murder.

"Well." Offering a polite head bob, Heath started to leave. "Good to see you."

She stopped him with a hand on his arm. "I would sure love a nice cold drink. And after the concert, dinner perhaps? I know the coziest little place down in Moreburg that serves thick, rare steaks and double baked potatoes."

A couple of weeks ago, he would have said yes. Something had changed, something that troubled him.

"I'm here with someone," he said, glad it was true. Michelle was beautiful and the type of woman he would have dated a year ago, but he simply wasn't interested. Not anymore.

"Oh." She pouted, an adorable pout that had doubtless worked on men all of her life. "What about our rain check?"

He removed her hand from his arm and gave the fingers a squeeze. His cell phone rang and, glad for the interruption, he said, "Excuse me," and pushed the talk button.

"Heath?" Cassie's voice sounded breathless. "I can't find you. I have to leave."

"I'm at the first aid station." His hand tensed on the smartphone. "What's wrong?"

"Can you take me home? I need to go to the hospital."

"The hospital?" Adrenaline surged into his bloodstream. With an apologetic glance, he turned his back on Michelle. Frantically, he searched the crowd for Cassie's familiar black hair and bright blue shirt. "Are your hurt? Sick? Talk to me."

"Annalisa is in labor."

"Meet me at the SUV."

She hadn't expected Heath to come with her, but, after making sure the auxiliary officers had everything under control, he'd insisted on heading straight to Fayetteville to the hospital. In his Expedition.

When they'd arrived at Regional Medical Center and started across the parking lot, Cassie paused. "You don't have to go inside."

"Want me to leave?"

"No, I'm glad you came." The admission surprised her. "But I don't want you to feel obligated, either. Driving me this distance was above and beyond the call of duty."

They paused at the crosswalk to let a car pass. The hospital was large and busy. One ambulance was pulling away as another came in. People entered and exited, some in street clothes, others in medical scrubs with security name badges on their chests.

"This isn't duty, Cassie. I'm here because I want to be. If you'll let me, I'd like to stay."

When Heath reached for her hand, Cassie was glad for the contact. Her fingers were cold against his hard warmth. Secure. Safe. "I'd be glad for the company."

"Look at you," he chided softly. "You're all shaky. Good thing I didn't let you drive yourself. You wouldn't want to end up in a ditch on a dark, lonely stretch of road."

The reminder of their first meeting brought a fleeting smile, but worry nagged too much to joke. "Annalisa is only eight months along. Do you think the baby is all right?"

His eyebrows raised. "Like I'm an expert?"

She huffed a short laugh that had absolutely no effect on her jitters. "Me, either. All I know about childbirth is what I've learned standing over women's hair. The stories are terrifying."

"Fifty hours of hard labor with no anesthesia and only a rusty bullet to bite down on?"

"Close enough."

"I've been with my brothers a couple of times when their kids were born." He stood to one side and let her enter the building first. "Everything went fine, but they were basket cases."

As Cassie stepped into the entry, cool air from overhead vents prickled the skin on her arms. She rubbed at them, belly jumping with nerves for her family.

"That's why I'm here. Austin will need me, even if he doesn't realize it yet. He is so in love with Annalisa, if anything should go wrong, he'll crumble."

"Did he say anything was wrong?" Heath punched the elevator button. A pair of passing nurses gave him the once-over before exchanging grins, though he seemed oblivious.

"No, his call was brief. He said she was admitted and in labor and he was waiting on the OB-GYN to arrive."

"Then say a prayer, and don't borrow trouble."

"Right." Heath wasn't a man who talked a lot about his faith but she knew he believed. Prayer and faith was the right direction, no matter what the problem.

"That's exactly what I'll do." It was what she'd already

done all the way to Fayetteville, but until Annalisa and baby were declared fit, she'd keep on praying.

They rode the elevator to the designated birthing floor, finding Austin without having to ask at the desk. The big, good-looking cowboy was standing outside a room talking to a doctor clad in green scrubs.

"He looks worried." She grabbed for Heath's hand, aware that she'd repeatedly clung to him today. Right now she wasn't even going to question the reasons. He was here and he made her feel better. Enough said.

"He's a first-time father. Of course he's worried. Midnight feedings, kindergarten, buying a car when the kid's sixteen, prom night, paying for college, and then there's the rehearsal dinner at the wedding." Heath raised his free hand in exclamation. "A man could go nuts."

He was joking to ease her tension and Cassie loved him for it. "You're pretty handy in a scary situation, you know that, Officer?"

"That's me. Sworn to protect and serve."

He was a lot more than that, but she didn't say so. They approached Austin who saw them coming.

Her brother looked at her with a beleaguered expression and said in a haggard voice, "I'm glad you're here, sis. We're in trouble."

Chapter Nine

Cassie went into action. Like the natural caregiver she was, she slid in next to her brother's side and put her arm around his back. "What's going on?"

Austin dropped an arm over her shoulder, gripping it with a calloused hand. "They can't stop her labor, and it's too early."

Cassie gazed toward the physician who looked hardly old enough to be out of college. He was a big guy, fresh-faced, blond and blue-eyed with peach fuzz for whiskers. "Are Annalisa and the baby in danger?"

"We're keeping a close watch. Baby is small but appears big enough to be viable."

She hated words like *viable*. This was a baby boy, a person, her nephew. Viable sounded so...so...medical. "What about Annalisa? Is her blood pressure the problem?"

"So far so good. We're monitoring everything and at this point, letting nature take its course. Should anything change, we have staff on hand ready to act."

"So the baby is going to be born tonight?"

"Looks that way."

A zing of fear-tinged exhilaration shot through Cassie.

Tonight she'd meet her brother's son. Her nephew. The first grandchild in their family.

"How much longer?"

The doctor's smile was sympathetic. "A while. She's in the early stages."

"Can we stay with her?"

"Absolutely. She'll need you. Especially you, Austin. Give Annalisa plenty of support and encouragement, and try not to worry too much."

Easy for him to say.

"I'll be in the hospital. Let the nurses know if you need anything. Okay?" The young doctor offered a reassuring smile.

"Will do." Austin held out his hand. "Thanks, Doc."

Cassie could feel the slight tremble in her brother's body as she moved away from his side. Austin was cowboy tough but Annalisa was his Achilles' heel. She'd brought him out of his reclusive shell, helped him find his way back to the Lord and had given him all the love missing in his first marriage. He was mush with her. Cassie had always found that sweet and endearing, a clue to the deep, caring man that was her brother. Tonight, it worried her. If anything should happen to another wife—

She cast the ugly thought into her mental trash can. They were all praying. Annalisa would be fine. So would baby boy.

As the doctor walked briskly away, Austin offered his hand to Heath. "Good of you to come with her, Heath. Thanks."

"Glad to." Heath shot a teasing grin at Cassie. "I'm not a big bluegrass fan anyway."

"She dragged you to that, huh?"

Cassie gave Heath a soft punch on the arm. "You love it, and you know you do. Both of you."

Austin's mouth lifted at the corners, but his eyes didn't smile. As much as they wanted to distract him, he was too worried about his family. "Ready to go in the room? I don't like to leave her alone. I only came out to talk to the doc in private."

"Were you afraid of what he might say?"

"Yeah." He ran his fingers through his hair. "I hate this. I hate seeing her scared and in pain. I want to punch something."

"Hang in, Austin." Heath clapped him on the shoulder. "I've stood beside my brothers in your shoes. They both vow that the end result is worth it."

"She wants this baby so bad." He looked sheepish. "Me, too."

"And you'll have him, safe and sound. Stop worrying," Cassie said. "Did you call Mom and Dad?"

"They're trying to get a flight out, but you know how that goes. Can't get here until tomorrow. Dad said they might drive, but that's at least six hours without sleeping first. With Dad's bad back, I told him to wait until tomorrow when they're fresh."

"Good idea. The baby will be here by then and they can spoil him while you and Annalisa rest."

"Yeah. Let's hope. Unless—"

"Hey, stop that. No 'unless' to it." Cassie leaned her face close to his, willing him to be positive. His first marriage had left him doubting the goodness in life. Annalisa, and his newfound faith, had done a lot to change that but tonight fear gripped him. "Everything is going to be okay. You hear me? You've put your life in God's hands. He's got your back."

"She's right, Austin," Heath said. "Baby will be here by morning, and you'll forget about this anxiety."

Austin drew a deep breath through his nose and nodded. "I'm counting on that."

"Come on, then." Heath clapped him on the shoulder again. "Let's go say hello to your beautiful wife. And I'll tell you about the time my brother fainted in the delivery room. No joke. Big, tough street cop. Bam! Out like a light."

Cassie watched in admiration as the new Whisper Falls police officer soothed her brother with his wit and charm and calm demeanor. Her heart turned over in her chest. The man had a way about him.

They entered the birthing unit where Annalisa was connected to several monitors and an IV. The machines ticked and beeped in a regular rhythm, and the filtering system pumped out the smell of cool, ionized air and clean sheets. Annalisa's eyes were closed but the moment the door swished, she opened them and turned her head. "Austin." She reached a hand over the metal bars.

Her brother was at his wife's side instantly to kiss her forehead and murmur something Cassie couldn't hear.

"What did the doctor tell you?" Annalisa's face was shiny with moisture. Anxiety and discomfort wrinkled her forehead.

Austin smoothed the lines with his fingertips. "The doctor says everything's fine. We're fixin' to have a baby, sweetheart."

"Oh, Austin." Then a contraction must have started because she closed her eyes, face tight, and began to take slow, deep breaths the way she'd learned in the countless videos they'd all watched.

Austin counted, encouraging her, talking in the sweetest manner. Cassie's insides squeezed at her brother's tender love for his wife.

Thank You, Lord, for bringing her into his life. Keep

them in Your loving hands tonight. Give them the beautiful, healthy baby they want so much.

She glanced at Heath who was watching them, too, a curious light in his eyes. To her surprise, she was holding his hand again. She didn't know when that had happened, but the connection brought comfort.

When the contraction ended, Annalisa opened her eyes, spotting Cassie and Heath. "Hey, you two. Stop hiding by the door. Come in here and make me laugh."

"Tell us if we're in the way or when you need privacy," Cassie said. "We can hang out in the lobby."

"Stay. At least for now. When things heat up, I may not want anyone around to hear me blasting Austin for causing this."

"Hey!" Austin pretended insult.

She squeezed his forearm. "You know I'm kidding. I wouldn't change places with any woman in the world right now no matter what. We've waited a long time for our little prince to come. All I want is for him to be strong and healthy."

"Me, too, babe, but I have a feeling it's going to be a long night for you."

And it was. For hours, between nurse and doctor visits, the four of them played card games and told stories until Annalisa became too uncomfortable to participate. By midnight, the patient was tiring fast. To give the couple some time and privacy in these last hours, Cassie and Heath found an open snack bar. Only one other person occupied a table.

"Sorry about your pizza," Heath said as they sat down at the empty table with machine sandwiches and cold drinks.

"Oh, you're not getting out of it that easy, mister. You still owe me a pizza."

"Good."

"Good? Why would you say that?"

"Because you'll have to go out with me again."

Cassie's heart jumped. She stared at him across her chilly ham and cheese. "Go out? As in a date?"

"Got a problem with that?"

Did she? Darrell floated into her consciousness along with Heath's accusation that her late husband was dirty. How could she possibly date him? But she already was, in a manner of speaking. She looked forward to seeing him. Wanted to talk to him, be with him, hear his opinion. Was she betraying Darrell's memory?

Oblivious to the churning doubts in her head, Heath said, "Someday I want to take you out for a real meal."

Okay, safe ground. She tried to look aghast. "As in healthy stuff? Don't you dare!"

They both laughed, breaking the tension. He was joking, being his usual easy self. But a real date with Heath Monroe sounded…nice. She wanted to dress up and go somewhere swanky on the arm of this man.

And she was starting to scare herself.

"I'm getting tired," she said, blinking away the grit in her eyes. Fatigue was the only excuse for her bizarre attraction to Heath tonight.

"All things considered, why wouldn't you be? Work all day, support your expecting brother all night."

"Don't forget I have to entertain you, as well."

"Am I work?"

More than he could ever know. "You've been great, Heath. I don't know what…" She let the words drift off, not wanting to say too much. Her emotions were a tangled mess she hadn't sorted out. Inside, a war raged between honoring Darrell and falling for Heath.

The thought brought her up short. Falling for him? No, no, she was just tired and emotional.

She laid aside the tasteless white-bread sandwich, surprised to find her food nearly eaten. She'd been hungrier than she'd realized. "I'm done."

"You look done," Heath said in a wry voice. "Done in. Come on." Heath scooped up their trash and deposited it before pulling out her chair. "You can lie down in the waiting room and catch a nap. I'll keep watch over brother and wife."

She could get used to his Texas manners. "What about you?"

"Lawmen don't need sleep."

"Ah, yes, the guardian. Protector of women and children and old ladies crossing the street."

"Don't forget puppies and kitties." His cute smile wrapped around her like a warm wind.

She definitely needed rest.

Curled up on a sofa in the waiting area, Cassie dreamed muddled dreams of Darrell and Heath and a crying baby on a Mexican beach. She woke with a start, pulse banging. The dreams weren't particularly frightening but something was wrong. Something she couldn't quite remember.

"Cassie." Heath's mellow voice sounded urgent. "Are you awake?"

"I am now." Sitting up, she pushed at her hair, aware of how she must look. One glimpse of Heath and she forgot all about her disheveled appearance. "What's wrong?"

"There's a problem with the baby. The doctor's talking to Austin and Annalisa now."

"A problem? Oh, dear God." Adrenaline shot through her veins stronger than a triple espresso. Panicked, she grabbled for Heath's hand, clinging. "What is it? Is he—"

"His heart rate is too low. They're talking about a C-section."

"Okay. Okay. A C-section. That's no big deal these days. Right?" She took a deep breath, trying to get her bearings. "I can't think yet. I was dreaming…"

"It's okay. Sorry to awaken you like that."

Cassie put her fingertips on her forehead. She was usually calm and alert in emergencies. Must be the strange, misty dream. "What time is it?"

"Three in the morning." He glanced toward the double doors and stood. "Here's Austin now."

Cassie ran to her brother. "Is she all right? What's happening?"

"I only have a minute. We're doing a C-section. I have to gown up."

"They're letting you go in?" Heath sounded as surprised as she was.

"Yes." Her brother's face was taut and pale with fear. "I won't let her go through this without me."

Tears welled in Cassie's eyes. "I love you, Austin."

"Love you, too. Pray for us." Then he was gone, striding in his long, cowboy stride toward his wife and son and a medical emergency.

Heath alternately prayed and reassured Cassie, trying to ease her worry with a conversation about outrageous baby names such as Pickle and Hashtag. To her credit, she'd come back with some doozies. Karaoke, for one, had made him snort.

She was a gamer, trying to remain upbeat, but her gaze drifted to the doorway over and over again. She loved her brother the way he loved his, and that counted big-time with him. Family was everything. Though he'd never been in her situation, he could empathize.

When a nurse in surgical attire pushed through the doorway, they both leaped to their feet.

"Annalisa?" The anxiety in Cassie's voice hurt him. Like Austin earlier, he wanted to punch something. Or better yet tuck her close to his chest and hold her. His suspect's widow was messing with his head.

The nurse smiled. "She did great. So did Daddy. Baby will be in the nursery in a few minutes."

"He's all right?" Cassie was squeezing Heath's hand so hard, his fingers were numb, and he didn't even care.

"Five pounds and four ounces of healthy outrage." She smiled again. "Wait until you hear that cry."

"He's all right. Heath, they're both okay." Before he knew what she was about, Cassie flung herself against his chest.

What else could a man do? He wrapped his arms around her and held her exactly the way he'd imagined.

Cassie didn't know what had come over her but being in Heath's embrace was amazing. She was a little embarrassed by her behavior, but by the time she'd regained her wits and backed away, pulse thudding like shoes in a clothes dryer, word came that the newborn was in the nursery. She dragged Heath out of the waiting room and rushed down the hall to the wide glass panes. She'd worry about the hug later.

A row of tiny swaddled babies lined the nursery. Inside, near the back, Austin stood beside a nurse peering into an Isolette. The cowboy's big hands were inside the crib, tending his son while the nurse looked on, her mouth moving. When Cassie and Heath approached the window, her brother looked up. The smile he gave them was one of relief and joy and not a little pride.

Cassie grinned hard enough to break her jaw and pointed to the baby and then to herself, indicating her desire to see him. With endearing awkwardness, her brother lifted his naked son in his huge hands and turned him toward the window. A wrinkled face puckered into an annoyed cry. The tiny arms and legs jerked inward.

"Oh, my goodness." Cassie pressed closer to the pane, snapping photos with her cell phone. "He's beautiful. Look at him, Heath. He's wonderful. So tiny and tough and precious."

"Your brother is a blessed man."

"Blessed," Cassie murmured, thinking Heath used exactly the right word. With uncharacteristic neediness, she battled the urge to lean her head on the lawman's sturdy, dependable shoulder. He was as close as a whisper, his side touching hers, his warmth seeping through her skin. If he turned his head, they'd be nose to nose. Mouth to mouth.

Something powerful turned over in her chest.

Bewildered, she refocused on her nephew and watched Austin minister to his son's needs and then slip out of the nursery and head toward Annalisa's room. Cassie and Heath remained at the window, watching the infant sleep. Now swaddled in a blue print blanket, baby boy Blackwell wore a stretchy blue stocking cap. Precious beyond words.

The heaviest emotion engulfed Cassie. A powerful yearning for more than a successful salon and a lot of great friends. An undeniable pull stretched from her to Heath. She pressed against the cool nursery window, stunned by the tsunami of emotions brought on by one baby's birth. She closed her eyes, drifted, aware of the man at her side, of the baby in the nursery, of the empty places in her heart.

"Cassie." Heath's voice was quiet.

"Hmm?" She was, she realized with a start, about to fall asleep against the cool window pane.

"You're tired. I should get you home."

Tired? She was out on her feet. She must be to keep having these aberrant thoughts about her life. About Heath.

Tomorrow, after a long sleep, she'd be back to her old self and feel differently.

"Home sounds wonderful. I am exhausted and you must be, too, but let's see Annalisa for a second first, okay?"

"Whatever you want."

"I don't even think that's possible."

He tilted his head. "Excuse me?"

She wanted a baby of her own. She wanted him. "Nothing. I'm getting delirious. We should go."

She started to walk away but Heath caught her arm and pulled her back. "Is something wrong?"

Everything. Nothing.

Stunned at her crazy thoughts, Cassie shook her head. "I'm too tired to think. I want to see my sister-in-law, and I want to go home and sleep for a week."

He studied her for a long moment as if he could see through her head and read her mind.

"I think I can arrange that." The corners of his mouth curled. "Except for the week of sleep which sounds pretty good to me, too. Good, but impossible with our work schedules."

Cassie raised her cell phone for one more snap of the sleeping infant. "I'm totally in love."

The words, softly spoken, took on a new meaning with Heath at her side. She swallowed down the stark, hungry yearning. She could love her nephew. She could love her family. But romantic love was not part of the deal. Not with a man who believed the worst about Darrell.

The sky was beginning to lighten by the time Heath drove the last quarter mile down Cassie's driveway. She'd dozed off several times during the trip but jerked awake as frustrated as a wet cat to have fallen asleep.

"You need me to keep you alert," she claimed. "I'm too tired to drag you out of a ditch tonight."

He didn't tell her he'd trained his body to sleep when it could and stay alert the rest of the time. He'd worked plenty of night shifts and twenty-four-hour days. Instead, he'd laughed at her and called her sleepy head. What he'd really meant was sleeping beauty. More than once, he'd glanced at her dozing profile, propped against the passenger window, and wondered what was happening between them. There was more than an investigation going on here. The trouble was he didn't know how to get around the fact that he'd started dating her to extract information. There was nothing wrong with subterfuge in the line of duty, and yet he felt compromised, conflicted…and as low as a snake's belly.

He rubbed a hand down his face and turned the A/C vent up a notch to keep alert.

He cared for her and it was eating him alive. The man in him wanted to come straight out and tell her the whole story. The agent in him held back.

He still didn't know if she'd been involved with her husband in drug trafficking. He didn't want to believe the worst, but that was his heart talking.

She was loyal, he'd grant her that. Either loyal or culpable and covering her tracks.

He hissed through his teeth, frustrated.

He hated thinking this way. Hated that he'd become so jaded about other human beings that he had trouble sorting the good guys from the bad.

Cassie was dedicated to clearing Darrell and to her memories of one of the shortest marriages on record. He hoped that was all, because a man like him understood that kind of loyalty. Understanding didn't make the truth of the situation any clearer.

"Hey, lazy," he said softly as he put the vehicle into

park. When she didn't move, he unbuckled his seat belt and leaned across to touch her shoulder. "Want me to carry you inside?"

Eyes closed, she nodded. "Mmm."

He'd been teasing, but the notion kick-started his heart. Why not? What would it hurt? Relief-fueled exhaustion had knocked her out cold.

Heath eased out of the driver's seat and went around to lift her into his arms. Austin's ranch dogs—the lab and the shepherd—ambled up, tails wagging as they sniffed his pants leg. He gave each a friendly pat before scooping up his passenger.

Cassie was thinner than he'd realized and easy to carry. When she snuggled against him like a child, his thudding pulse served as a reminder. This was not his little niece dozing after he'd taken her to a Disney movie. This was a woman who did crazy things to his head. A woman who might be involved in drug trafficking. His job was to find out what she knew, no matter the means and no matter how she moved him.

And he'd never disliked his vocation as much as he did this moment.

At the house, he lowered her to the porch swing, bracing the wooden structure with his shoulder and leg to stop the sway. "Sorry, Sleeping Beauty. I don't have a key to your house."

"What?" Muzzy headed, she opened her eyes and glanced around, her voice thick and confused. "How did I get here? Are we home?"

"Home."

He sat down beside her and pulled her sleep-lazed body close to his side. For support, he told himself, until she was fully awake. Feminine, soft, she smelled of sunshine and salon shampoo and something quintessentially Cassie. "The sun will be up soon. Want to wait for it?"

"Mmm. Sounds beautiful." She gave a great, heaving sigh and settled deeper against him.

Something tenderized inside him, a mallet driving out the hardened spots. He stroked the side of Cassie's face, smoothed her hair and waited for the sunrise.

Cassie awakened with a smile. Someone was touching her hair. Someone warm and gentle and male. Or maybe she was dreaming again, though the moment felt real. If only he would kiss her, the way he used to do. The way she hadn't been kissed in a very long time.

She put her arms around his neck and lifted her face. "Kiss me," she whispered.

His body went still. In the breaking dawn she couldn't read his face, but she heard the sharp intake of breath. "Are you sure?"

The pleasant rumble of his voice made her pulse dance. "Mmm. Very."

Wide hands caressed her face with the greatest care and then slid into her hair before he touched his lips to hers. The kiss was tentative, questioning as though he held himself in check. As sweet and tempting as a hot fudge sundae. Cassie burrowed in, kissing him back. The kiss lengthened and one became two. So nice. So wonderful. Her chest filled with a beautiful pleasure. For a brief moment—too brief—his arms tightened and then he released her and pulled away.

"The sun is rising over the mountains," he said softly.

Cassie roused herself from the languor, increasingly aware of her surroundings. A warm flush eased up the back of her neck. What in the world had come over her? She'd kissed Heath. And she'd liked it.

"I'm sorry," she said, and pushed to her feet. Her whole body felt weak and heavy.

"Don't be. The sunrise is beautiful."

He'd intentionally misunderstood. Though he was right, of course. The May sun peeked lemon-yellow above a layered sea of gold and coral that drifted above the deep green of the woods. In seconds, brilliant light spoked the sky illuminating a scatter of dark clouds from the inside out. It was a poet's sky, a dreamer's morning. She thought of her songwriter friend, Lana, and hoped she was awake and watching.

As for Cassie, her fatigue was too great, and her brain was cloudier than the heavens. "Gorgeous, but I'm too tired to enjoy it."

"Go on, then. Get some rest," Heath said gently, placing one last kiss on her forehead. "Aunt Cassie."

The new term brought a smile as Heath dropped his hands and turned, stepping off the porch.

She wanted to call him back and explain, but what would she say? *I was sleepy. I kissed you by mistake.* Because in her heart of hearts, she was afraid that wasn't true.

Bemused, bewildered and yearning, Cassie closed the door to the empty, silent house. She didn't go to bed. Not yet. She went to the window and pulled aside the curtain. She watched as the dome light flared inside Heath's SUV, a flash of shadowy light. Her throat filled at that one last glance of Heath's face before he started the SUV and drove away.

Tootsie tapped in from the hallway and rubbed against her legs. Cassie scooped her up and held the fuzzy little poodle against her cheek before letting her out to do her business.

She was overtired. That was all. She wouldn't have kissed him otherwise. Would she?

Disloyalty tugged at her.

Darrell was gone. Heath was alive and real and she might be falling for him, as impossible as that seemed.

"Lord, this is crazy. I'm worn down. Overemotional. The new baby and all." She sucked in her bottom lip. "Oh, Jesus, I always wanted a baby."

Tears prickled her eyes. She was definitely exhausted. Things would seem different after a few hours' sleep.

Chapter Ten

He was losing his edge. And he knew better. Heath had seen it happen too many times. A cop fell for the wrong woman and she took him down.

But try as he might, he couldn't keep Cassie out of his head. The snap of green eyes, the slash of bright red lips curved in a mischievous grin, the sweet and sassy depth of personality. A man who claimed Cassie as his woman would know a partner and friend, as well as a love. And oh, how she loved. He'd seen her with her family, her customers, her friends, her church. He knew her loyalty to her husband's memory. Cassie loved them all with a passion as warm as an Ozark summer.

After sleeping most of Sunday away, Heath had given in to the urge and called her. He'd asked about the baby, kept it light, and never mentioned the devastating kiss. Neither had Cassie.

He'd phoned his mother, too, and then made two more calls to hassle Holt and Heston awhile. Granted, Heath was restless, troubled by circumstances of his own creation.

Now, late Monday morning, he drove the streets of Whisper Falls, combing the residential areas for an eighty-seven-year-old Alzheimer's patient who'd wandered away from his daughter's home.

On the dash, his father's badge glinted in the bright sunlight, an ever-present reminder of his calling. Yet he couldn't believe Cassie was involved with Louis Carmichael's drug business. Or maybe he didn't *want* to believe it. That was the trouble with relationships. They skewed a man's focus.

As he turned a corner onto Oak Street, he spotted an elderly man sitting beneath a tree across the street from the school. Children played on the playground, their voices carrying to him like a cheerful wind. Heath's chest tightened, both with relief at having found the man and at the poignancy of his location. That Elmer would come here, near a school, made perfect sense. The old gentleman had been a science teacher for many years.

After a confirmation glance at the photo on the seat beside him, Heath radioed the news to cancel the silver alert and whipped in next to the curb and got out, approaching the man.

"Elmer, are you okay?" Heath knelt on one knee next to the thin, withered old man. His clothes were smudged with dirt as if he'd fallen, and he smelled of arthritis rub. Compassion thickened Heath's throat. Someday, he or his loved ones might be in this position. "Sharon is worried about you."

"Sharon?" Elmer asked in a frightened voice. "What is this place? Everything looks different."

"Don't worry, sir. I'm a police officer. I'll take you home."

"That's nice of you, son." Though his rheumy eyes were clouded, Elmer's entire body sagged in helpless, hopeless relief. "Marjorie made a carrot cake this morning and I'm hungry. My wife is a fine, fine cook."

"Yes, sir." Heath helped the elderly man to his feet, keeping the sadness from his expression. Marjorie, he knew from the daughter's information, was his long-dead wife. "Let's get you home."

Within fifteen minutes, he'd returned Elmer to a greatly relieved daughter, feeling good about the outcome, but pity for the situation. Elmer was fortunate to have a loving daughter to care for him. Her role couldn't be easy.

Who would be there for him if Alzheimer's came calling someday?

As he sat inside his truck on a tree-lined street aching for a confused old man, his mind returned to the bone he'd been gnawing for days. Cassie Blackwell and her husband.

Holt had no news to share yet. Too early. He had a case to finish before he could leave for Mexico. Even then, a private investigator might not discover anything that wasn't already known. Nonetheless, Heath's instincts were strong and they told him something was hinky. The question was, did Cassie know? Was her professed cooperation and the file full of information a ruse? His instincts said no. But maybe his emotions were getting in the way again.

He never should have started this crazy thing with her. If she knew of his suspicions, that he'd begun seeing her as means to gather evidence, she'd hate him. In a way, that might be the best thing. Kick him to the curb and get it over with before more damage was done.

But Saturday had meant something special. In those moments when they'd watched the newborn boy together, he'd discovered a hole in his life, the missing link, so to speak. Family. Oh, he had Mom and the brothers and their terrific broods, but no one of his own. No one to make plans with. No one to dream dreams and build a life and have kids. No one to take care of him when he was old and frail.

He was thirty-six years old and he'd never wanted any of

that. All he'd ever cared about was taking out the bad guy, honoring Dad's memory, making the world a better place. He wasn't even sure he wanted it now, but those stunning minutes at the hospital and again on Cassie's front porch when she'd kissed him had Heath wondering if perhaps he was missing something important.

"Lord, I don't ask for much, but I could use some guidance."

Maybe he should turn the investigation over to the DEA and forget about it. No, too soon. Too little evidence, and in his arrogance, he wanted to solve the case for himself while protecting Cassie. The effort seemed on the verge of backfiring in his face.

Better call Holt again tonight and see if his brother could jumpstart things from Texas.

His radio crackled and he took a call from dispatch. A domestic dispute. Not his favorite call, but he radioed back and headed that direction.

"Isn't he the cutest baby ever?" Cassie stood above Tara Wilkin's head, painting highlights into her shoulder-length brown hair. Tara held a dozen photographs of Austin's new baby.

"A darling for certain. What did they name him?"

"Levi Austin. Annalisa insisted on naming him after his daddy, and I just love it."

"Adorable and very cowboy."

"Austin says Levi will be a bull rider. Annalisa says no way her baby is getting on a bull." Cassie smiled, remembering the cute argument the pair had had at the hospital.

"I think Annalisa will win that one," Tara said. "I can't imagine letting my son on a two-thousand-pound bull."

"Me, either!" Not that she had a son.

"Tell her who took you to the hospital and stayed until

the baby arrived." This from Louise whose rust-red hair looked electric-plug wild today.

"It's not a big deal, Louise. I didn't have my car."

"You could have gotten it."

"I was in a hurry."

"So apparently was your handsome hero in uniform who remained by your side *all* night."

A titter of excitement swept through the shop, a wave of speculation.

"Wait a minute," Cassie insisted, pointing the paint brush. "That sounds bad, but it wasn't. We were at the hospital all night waiting for the baby to arrive. Nothing happened."

Well, not exactly nothing, but not the kind of thing they were tittering about.

"Why is your face turning red?"

"It is not!" She spun toward the mirror. Sure enough, her cheeks glowed like a traffic light. "Y'all are embarrassing me. Heath and I are pals."

"Fiddlesticks," Miss Evelyn said, her fingertips deep in a soaking bowl. "Uncle Digger said the pair of you were giggling like teenagers at the Iron Horse the other day. Looked cozy and romantic over Cokes and fries."

Cassie groaned. She and Heath had been laughing about one of his dumbest criminal stories. He had a gazillion and they made her laugh like a loon. There was nothing romantic about it. Except when he'd touched her hair and told her she smelled good.

"You've been a widow long enough, Cassie," Tara said. "And if I had a hot-looking officer of the law in pursuit of me, I'd slam on my brakes and let him catch me."

The shop ladies howled with laughter. All Cassie wanted to do was slink away.

Louise lifted Miss Evelyn's hand from the soak solution.

"I'm here with you all day, Cassie, sugar. I know how you light up when Heath Monroe comes through that door. At least admit you like him for more than a friend. That old 'pals' story is getting stale."

"I do not light up."

"Do, too. Now, confess. We're your friends. We have a duty to know."

Cassie rolled her eyes. "If I do, will all of you stop badgering me?"

"No. We'll want details."

Another chorus of laughter. This time, Cassie clamped her mouth shut and concentrated on Tara's hair. Okay, so they were right. She had a thing for the new assistant police chief and it didn't feel a bit like friendship. Saturday night, or rather Sunday morning at sunrise, had pretty much sealed her fate. The frozen places had started to thaw. The numbness was giving way to feeling, something she'd never expected to happen. But her friends didn't understand the dilemma, didn't realize how risky and terrifying it was to step out of her comfort zone and cross the lines of friendship. The thought of giving her heart, maybe to lose it again, was scarier than climbing Whisper Falls during an ice storm. She didn't, however, say that to her friends.

After work Cassie walked out of the salon without so much as a glance toward the courthouse. She didn't look on the streets for Heath's big black Expedition, either.

She drove to Resthaven, a tidy, cedar-lined cemetery situated on the eastern edge of town. Her little Nissan probably knew the way by itself, she'd driven here so many times over the last three years. The gates never closed and the place was usually deserted and blessedly peaceful, especially at night with the stars overhead. Cassie knew because she had spent a few nights beside Darrell's gravesite in those early, pain-filled days.

A hearty wind whipped her hair as she approached the red granite headstone carved with Darrell's name. The wind carried the scent of cedar and newly mowed grass across the bright flowers and silent graves.

At the gravesite next to Darrell's, a small American flag *whap-whapped* in the breeze. At the foot, a bronze WWII marker proclaimed the dead to be a veteran like many others buried here in this peaceful vale. To her knowledge Darrell had never served, but she wasn't positive. They'd had so little time together. There were too many things she didn't know about her late husband. Would never know now. She'd never even met his family—if he'd had one other than Louis Carmichael.

She stroked her hand across the bumpy name carved in sun-warmed granite. "Why didn't I know more about your life? Was it because everything happened so fast? Or did you have secrets?"

Shame was an instant and sharp rebuke. She didn't want to believe the love of her life could have been involved in criminal activity, and yet Heath had made her doubt. She was ashamed of that. Ashamed of lost loyalty.

As she'd done dozens of times, she sat down on the cool grass and leaned against the headstone. In times past, she'd wept for all that had been lost. Today, she contemplated… and prayed.

A cardinal fluttered to the ground, a flash of color, like her favorite red lipstick. Darrell had bought it for her. He'd loved her in red, his favorite color.

"I still wear it," she told him, though only the cardinal heard.

Something niggled in the back of her mind. A faint memory she couldn't quite bring to the fore.

She had the sudden urge to drive out to Louis's trailer house. Darrell had lived there until the wedding. Some of his things were likely left behind in the rubble, though Louis had claimed the opposite and refused to let her look. She didn't know why the cousin had disliked her so much. But according to Heath, Louis had left, apparently before the storm, and hadn't been heard from since.

Maybe she'd find something her beloved had left behind, something to reassure her that Darrell had been the man she'd believed him to be.

The winding road grew narrower and less traveled with each passing mile as Cassie guided her car deep into the lush Ozark woods. Clouds of redbud trees lined the roadsides, sprinkling their lavender-red blossoms on her windshield. The only person on the remote ribbon of dirt, Cassie rolled down her window and breathed in the spring. A sweet, floral scent, higher pitched than peach but every bit as luscious, filled the interior of the car. Dogwood, perhaps?

When she approached a fork from which one way ambled off to the left like a cow path, Cassie knew the trailer site was near. Though she'd been to Louis's mobile home only once, she remembered the way because she and Darrell had lingered at this fork, had gotten out of the car and walked a ways holding hands, a romantic stroll.

Today she didn't stop the car, but the memory swamped her for a moment and moistened her eyes. Those had been good days, happy moments when the future seemed impossibly rosy. And indeed, it had been impossible. Only she hadn't known it then.

With a regretful sigh, she blinked away the moisture and followed the winding trail deeper into the trees until it dead-ended at the wreckage of a mobile home. She supposed she should have come sooner, when Heath had first told her about the tornado damage, but she'd been afraid of Louis.

The thought gave her pause as she stopped at the end of the rough-cut driveway. Louis had made her nervous, but until now, she'd never acknowledged the fear. He'd never been nice to her and had accused Darrell of selling out when they'd married. She still didn't understand what he'd meant by that.

As Cassie exited the car, an eerie silence hung over the abandoned place. It was as if the trees had eyes and knew the secrets hidden among the rubble. The trailer had been in bad shape before the storm, but now only sheet metal and the remains of Louis's life—and Darrell's—covered a long swath of ground. Even the well house had collapsed. The tank was gone, too, but not ripped away by the storm. The remaining pipes were too neatly cut.

Someone had taken the tank, probably to recycle or use it as their own. Hill families were often poor enough to scavenge, and she wondered what else had disappeared at the hands of looters.

The yellow police tape still surrounded a small area at the center, though a piece of tape would not deter treasure seekers. The wind in her hair, she gazed thoughtfully toward the place where Chief Farnsworth had found evidence that Darrell and Louis sold drugs. She still couldn't believe Darrell had known what his cousin was doing. When she'd been here that one time, she'd seen nothing out of the ordinary, other than a man who clearly did not want her there.

Careful to be on the lookout for copperheads and shards of glass and metal, Cassie moved through the debris. Here, the ground remained soggy from the heavy spring rains and repeated thunderstorms. They'd had more than their share this spring, so much that anything worth salvaging from Louis's trailer was likely ruined.

A cottontail bolted out from beneath a stuffed, upturned chair. Cassie yelped, throwing her hands out to the sides in alarm. The rabbit, as startled as she, rocketed into the overgrown grass and weeds. Cassie laughed at her skittishness, though several minutes passed before her pulse returned to normal.

She wasn't exactly afraid to be here, but the place gave her the creeps just as its owner had done.

"Why did I bother?" she muttered as she looked around and toed the rubble. There was nothing here. Nothing left that mattered. Heath and Chief Farnsworth would have removed anything of value, wouldn't they? Or was that not in the line of police work?

She stepped over a downed tree, disheartened and yet not ready to give up the search for some small bit of encouragement. A shiny object caught her eye, probably a gum wrapper or pop tab, but she walked toward it, wishing she'd changed her shoes before making this trip. Her heels stabbed holes in the soft ground. Given her respectful fear of snakes, she used a stick to push aside wet leaves and paper. A small gold-colored lid appeared. Cassie stared in bewildered surprise. Discovering the lid was as unsettling as finding a snake. She picked it up, growing more and more puzzled, for indeed she recognized the tube-shaped object…because it was hers.

"What is this doing here?" She turned the familiar tube over in her hands. This was the top to one of her lipsticks. She must have dropped it that one time Darrell had brought her here and argued with Louis.

She turned the lid over in her palm. Sun glinted off the metal. It was only a lipstick cover. There was nothing sinister about that, and yet she had the weirdest disquiet. Thanks to Heath's insinuations, she was tilting at windmills, imagining misdeed where none existed.

More focused now, she poked at the decaying leaves, turning them up along with bits of paper, broken shingles, and miscellaneous trash in search of the remaining lipstick case. With effort, she muscled a busted chest onto its side, spilling the contents from the drawers.

Why hadn't Louis salvaged any of his belongings before he'd left? Or had he left before the storm struck? Did he even know his house was in ruins? Where was he? Where would he have gone? Did he know the police wanted to question him?

Frustrated, she wished she'd known more about Darrell and his family. He'd always been vague. He was from out west and his parents were dead. That's all he'd ever said.

She pilfered through the chest, aware of the invasion of privacy. Cassie didn't care. If Darrell had left anything behind, it belonged to her, not Louis. If she could only find one little hint to prove Darrell was not involved in Louis's illegal activities.

A troubling thought appeared like a gnat in her ear, insisting on attention. She let it in, turning it over for examination. Why had Darrell come to a tiny rural community in the Ozarks in the first place? Was his cousin the only reason? He certainly hadn't come to claim a job opportunity as Heath had done. But hadn't she likewise wondered why a man of Heath's training would give up a federal agent position to play second banana in a small town police department?

Most of the chest held nothing but clothing items, most likely the reason Chief Farnsworth and Heath had left the chest and its contents behind. In the bottom drawer, beneath a T-shirt, she spied a small, folded piece of paper. Cassie opened the page…and her knees went weak.

"I love you," the note read in Darrell's tidy print. "For-

ever and always. You are the best thing that ever happened
to me. Tonight is too far away."

Below the sweet words, her handwriting responded,
"You are my breath, my every heartbeat. I can't believe I
finally found you. Thank you for loving me."

Sinking to the side of the rickety, broken chest, weak
as water, Cassie recalled the evening, after a busy day's
work, when she'd found the note on her windshield beneath
a wiper blade. Joy had burst inside her to be completely
loved, to be the beloved focus of this one, wonderful man.
That evening, she'd returned the note hidden inside a candy
bar she'd slipped into his pocket. It was the first of many
"secret" love notes they'd written to each other.

"But you kept the first one," she whispered, not caring
that moisture once again clouded her vision.

Regardless of what else he'd done, Darrell Chapman had
loved her. Of that one thing she was convinced.

When the wave of bittersweet memory passed, Cassie
continued her search though she had no idea what she was
after other than a lipstick tube which had no meaning. Seeing more papers stuck beneath a rumpled pile of rags, she
pulled them out and began sorting through. Clearly this had
been Darrell's dresser, or at least his drawer. Notes, old bills
and even a few maps of Mexico. Not unusual, given Darrell's love for the country's perfect diving beaches. She had
so little left that had belonged to him. Though the papers
were of no value to anyone else, these were things Cassie
wanted to keep.

She smoothed one of the maps open on her lap, recalling
the day they'd discussed their honeymoon and he'd showed
her where they would go, exciting her with stories of Mexico's beauty, of the sea and the fish, the beach and the sun.

Her finger went to the spot he'd circled in red. Playa Del
Carmen. Awash in memory of those three perfect days, she

hardly looked up when a big black SUV, glinting in the fading sun, rumbled down the driveway.

Heath's boots crunched on debris as he exited the Expedition, his attention on the woman sitting amidst the chaos, a handful of papers in her lap.

"Hi," he said, not wanting to startle her though she'd surely heard his approach.

She lifted her face then and his stomach dipped, that roller coaster drop he was starting to equate with each initial glance of Cassie. Memory of Saturday night, of the sweet companionship, the shared birth, and those troublesome kisses gripped him. His gaze, that misbehaving reaction, shot to her mouth before he could bring it under control.

"What are you doing out here?" Was that a blush on her cheekbones? Was she remembering, too?

"I was about to ask you the same thing." He stepped over a dirty, soggy pillow to reach her. Tears glistened on her lashes. He reached out, touched her cheek with only the tips of his fingers. Her skin was warm and moist. "Have you been crying?"

Her hand followed his, expression puzzled. "Have I?"

"Something's wrong. Tell me." His chest filled with the painful need to make things better and the sharp realization that by being himself, who he was called to be, who he *must* be, Heath could only make things worse for her. Wanting to hold her more than he should, Heath perched a hip on the sideways chest, found it sturdy enough, and settled next to her. They connected shoulder to knee, though not enough when he really wanted her in his arms. "What's upset you? Did you remember something?"

"If you mean pertinent to your case against Darrell, no. But I *was* remembering."

Ah, yes, of course. Remembering her late husband, that impossible competitor. Darrell had lived here. Maybe they'd even met here and spent time together in this place.

Then, the agent in him took charge and dropped an ugly suspicion into his brain. Why was Cassie here now? Had she driven to the trailer in an attempt to hide evidence he and Chief Farnsworth might have missed? He started to ask but didn't, not sure he wanted the answers. Not today with Saturday night as fresh in his mind as the scent of dogwood blossoms from the nearby woods. "You look sad. Am I intruding?"

"I'm okay. Just trying to sort through my thoughts. How did you know I was here?"

"A guess. I saw you drive out of town earlier but you never came back. Chief said you visited the cemetery often but you weren't there."

"I was there earlier. Then I got this wild idea to come here."

"What for?"

"I wanted to find something to make you understand. I needed to look."

A breath of fragrant breeze lifted a lock of her hair and set it dancing. Heath smoothed it down again. He loved her hair, sleek and black and as shiny as his new truck.

"And did you find anything?" He leaned over her shoulder, caught the scent of her hair salon and wished he wasn't suspicious of her coming here. He also wished they were two people who'd met outside of his job, away from the deceit and danger of the drug world that would not let him go. A map was spread on her lap and someone had made notations, circled places along the water's edge.

She shrugged. "A few clothes and papers that belonged to Darrell. They were in this chest. I guess you didn't take them as evidence because they weren't important."

"Chief searched the chest." She'd not mentioned anything of importance. "I see you found a map."

"Yes. A map of Mexico."

Heath's instincts went on police alert. "Darrell's or Louis's?"

She angled her face in his direction. Her clear green eyes were flecked with yellow, like pots of gold hidden in spring grass. He wanted to take her in his arms and forget all about the investigation, but the map could be important. The chief must have missed it somehow during her search, a fact that would infuriate her. But at one point, they'd experienced a cloudburst that had sent them running for their vehicles. It was the only reason he could imagine for the chief's misstep. She would never have intentionally disregarded anything related to Mexico.

"Darrell's. He showed it to me before our honeymoon." She tapped a spot. "See? Where he circled the city?"

He saw more than that on the map and wondered if she knew. Frustrated to have missed this piece of evidence, he suppressed the desire to snatch the map from her fingers.

"I found some other things, too," Cassie went on, her voice soft. "A note he sent me. It's kind of personal."

"You don't have to show it to me." Truth was he didn't want to see it. He didn't want to read another's man personal notes to this woman.

"I'd like for you to see it. Then maybe you'll believe what I do, that Darrell would never have done anything to hurt me."

"I never said he would have."

"You implied that our trip to Mexico was more than a honeymoon."

He had, and he still believed his assumption was correct. Cassie knew it, too. He could see the hurt lurking in those fascinating eyes and was sorry. Sorry she'd married

Darrell. Sorry he'd gotten personally involved with a suspect's widow. Sorry if this turned out to be more heartache for both of them.

"All right. What do you have?"

Heath hoped she had proof of her husband's innocence… and hers. It would make his sleep much more restful.

Cassie handed him an ordinary sheet of paper, and the cop in him immediately wondered if the document contained useable prints. He'd found no Darrell Chapman in the database but fingerprints might resolve that.

"Go ahead. Read it."

He skimmed what was essentially a love note between the two of them, nothing useful in an investigation, but painfully romantic to read. "I'm not sure how this proves anything, Cassie."

"Don't you see? Darrell loved me. I was his everything."

"And he was yours," he said. What was happening that he was jealous of a dead man?

Cassie said nothing, but continued to stare at him, willing him to accept what evidence denied. He couldn't.

"Anything else?" he asked quietly and saw her disappointment. It was there in the drop of her shoulders, the downward curve of her enchanting red mouth, the cool retreat in her eyes. He'd dashed her hope, a terrible thing to do.

"Just this." Her reply was despondent as she turned a palm up and parted her fingers. A bronze/gold tube flashed in the sunlight.

Heath's radar started to whirr. Proceeding with caution, careful not to touch the tube, he said, "What's this about?"

"A lid to my lipstick. I found it over there." She pointed to a pile of rubble similar to dozens of other piles. "I must have left it here the one time Darrell brought me out to meet Louis."

"Do you have one missing?"

"I'm not sure." She frowned, pursed her lips. Ah, those distracting lips. "Not that I recall but I have several of this brand."

"Would you object to my keeping it for a while, along with the maps?"

Cassie recoiled, closing her fingers around the tube. "Why?"

"Police business." *Fingerprints, drug residue, to study what I see on that map.* "In an investigation, we like to look at everything."

"These are personal, Heath. There is nothing to investigate. Chief Farnsworth would have taken them if they were pertinent."

"Will you trust me on this, Cassie?" He held out an upturned palm. "I promise to get them back to you as soon as possible."

She hesitated so long he thought he might have to demand them, something he didn't want to do. He was walking a tightrope in this case already, that fine line between caring for Cassie and his code of ethics. In fifteen years in law enforcement, he'd never been this personally involved with a potential suspect, never been this close to walking away from what he believed in, what he'd lived for since he was twelve years old.

His father's badge burned against his thigh, a symbol of dedication and honor. Was Heath Monroe about to become a bad cop, because of a woman?

"Cassie," he urged. "Please."

She gnawed at her lip, eyes worried. "I'll get them back?"

"You will."

She placed the map, the tube, and the letter in his hand. "I'm trusting you."

"I know." And that was the crux of the matter. He was secretly investigating her. And she trusted him.

Chapter Eleven

Cassie was in a strange mood when she left the tornado site, but Heath had offered to buy pizza and she couldn't pass that up. Torn between loyalty to Darrell and attraction to Heath, she was in turmoil. Not that she still clung to Darrell's memory like some wan heroine in a Southern novel who grows old and dies still mourning her loss, but that she felt a certain responsibility to preserve her late husband's good name.

"I'm in no hurry to go home," she told Heath inside the oregano-scented Pizza Pan. "Austin and Annalisa need some time alone with the new baby. I'm sure they'd prefer I make myself scarce for a while."

She needed the distraction, as well. Too often of late, her sleep was disturbed by spinning thoughts and jack-rabbit memories she couldn't quite pin down.

A video game played by a pimply teen whirred and clanged and flashed lights as he racked up points destroying space invaders. The greasy smell of cheese—her favorite smell in the universe next to the salon—permeated the vinyl booth.

"Did they tell you that?"

"No, they wouldn't. But I'm trying to be sensitive." She

smiled. "They haven't had much time alone since they married, thanks to *moi*."

"When did they come home from the hospital?"

"Last night." She fiddled with the plastic straw poked through a lid into the ice and Coke. "I've been thinking of getting an apartment."

"Yeah? Why?"

"Oh, you know." She fluttered her fingers. "They're a family now, and I'm in the way." Well, didn't that sound pathetic and whiney?

"Have you talked to your brother about this?"

"Of course not, silly. He'd deny it, and it's just a feeling I've had lately."

He picked up one of her fingers and rubbed the back of it. The connection soothed, as he'd intended. Heath was good at that. Soothing. "Why not wait it out, spend some time with your new nephew first? See how things go in the next few weeks or months."

"Maybe." She wasn't sure of anything lately. She, a confident businesswoman, one of the movers and shakers in Whisper Falls, had lost her self-assurance.

She looked at the strong, steady, masculine finger fiddling with her turquoise nail. Did Heath have something to do with this restlessness? She was afraid of that answer, afraid he did, afraid he had tilted her world. Like Louis's trailer, tipped on its side and shaken, her neat, tidy life was flying apart since the night she'd followed an SUV down a ravine and met Heath Monroe.

"If you ever decide to go apartment hunting…" He let the offer ride.

"Maybe I should do that. Check out my options."

"It might make you feel better, not that I think Annalisa and Austin are trying to dump you." He pushed his Coke to the side. "I mean, come on. Why would they? Built-in babysitter."

She laughed, his intention, no doubt. "Babysitter. Doting aunt. I gladly play both rolls. But I *would* like to look at apartments and small houses and see what's available. Darrell and I visited some places on the bluff but he was leaning toward a trailer in the country like Louis's."

"You never rented an apartment together?"

"Whirlwind romances don't have time for that, Heath. Darrell said something would work out when we returned from Mexico." She pulled the straw from the cup, sucked the end of it. "In a sad way, he was right."

"The chief set me up with my apartment, but I think there are a couple of others on the same street. Small but nice. Not too hard on the wallet."

"Really?" She perked up. Maybe the change was what she needed. "I want to see them."

"Then let's do it. Tomorrow after work?" He lifted one eyebrow. "And after we could grab chili dogs and cheese fries."

With a laugh, Cassie put a hand to her chest. "You sweet talker. I'm in!"

By the time she arrived at the ranch, the sun had disappeared, the porch light was on and the two faithful dogs didn't bother to get off the porch to sniff and circle. Like a set of furry bookends, one lay at each side of the door, long tails thumping the wood floor.

"Vicious beasts," she said, slowing to pat each head before letting herself inside.

Heath had kissed her good-night again. And she'd let him. Had wanted him to. She could still feel that whisper soft brush of skin against her mouth, the tickle of his facial hair. Gentle and sweet and a tad of dark passion he restrained so beautifully.

Other than Tootsie, the poodle, the living room was empty, but a high-pitched wail of angry infant came from down the hall. Tootsie raised up on Cassie's leg, shiny button eyes beseeching.

Cassie scooped her up. "Unless you and I can find another home, you'll have to get used to it, Toots. Babies cry."

Boy, did this one ever cry.

Cassie followed the sound down the hall to the nursery she and Annalisa had prepared. The room was both pretty and masculine in the palest brown and baby blue. "Master Levi is not a happy boy. What did you do to him?"

She was kidding, but Annalisa wasn't in the mood for jokes.

"Nothing. I don't know." Her usually perfect hair was disheveled and there was a major milk stain on her robe. "Why is he crying so much?"

"Don't look at me. I can fix his hair." *And yours,* but she wasn't about to say that tonight. "After that I'm lost."

"Me, too." Annalisa's gorgeous blue eyes were vexed and worried. The puffiness in her face had subsided but the fatigue had not.

"Let me do something. I don't know what *he* needs, but *you* need to rest. Where is my pig-hearted brother?" She would tear a strip off him for leaving Annalisa alone. The woman had just experienced childbirth and surgery!

"He went into town."

"Town! What for?" Cassie was indignant. How dare he?

Annalisa offered a wan smile. "You look as if you'll wring his neck."

"I will. I can't believe he'd leave you this way. Where did he go? The feed store? The jerk. You've had surgery. You need help." She rushed to her sister-in-law's side and took the baby. Levi felt as light as a hairbrush. But softer and more flexible. Scary flexible, like a bundle of warm towels.

"Don't be mad at Austin." Annalisa smiled a little, sheepish as she shuffled toward the padded rocker. The expensive handmade rocker Austin had bought from an Ozark wood craftsman. "He went to the store for me. I craved mint chocolate-chip ice cream."

That took the fire out of Cassie's smokestack. "Oh. Well, in that case, I'll let him live another day." She pulled Levi Austin close to her chest and cooed, "There now, my little man. Let Aunt Cassie fix it."

The baby squinched his eyes tight and screamed. That was a seriously red face.

"Is it time for him to eat?" she asked over the wail.

"Just fed him."

"Tummy ache?"

"I don't know how to tell."

"Me, neither." Cassie had run the gamut of her baby knowledge but she understood women and Annalisa was pale and wobbly. "You look like you're about to pass out. Go to bed. I can handle him until Austin gets back."

"Are you sure?"

"Go."

"Call me if you get tired of dealing with him."

"Go."

Like an old lady, a slightly bent Annalisa held to her incision and shuffled across the hall to the room she shared with Austin. She left the door open, an action Cassie found endearing. Annalisa's mother instinct was strong. No matter how weak and tired, she'd be back in an instant if Cassie didn't find a way to soothe her baby.

Rocking and cooing and saying completely stupid things to a crying baby who couldn't have cared less, Cassie walked back and forth across the floor. This was the way things would be if she had a child. The way of a new mother, anxious to do the right thing and not knowing what that was. Feeling her way in the dark, hoping for the best, trusting God to get her through.

At the moment, that was the story of Cassie's life. As if the tornado had swept through Whisper Falls and torn away the protective cocoon she'd been hiding in for three years. Maybe longer.

She shifted the baby to her shoulder and patted his back, careful to support his downy bobble head. With his sweet breath warm on her neck, she hummed "Blessed Assurance"—something she needed more of—and slowly, slowly Levi's cries shuddered to a halt.

"Thank You, Lord," Cassie murmured, nearly limp with gratitude and relief.

She patted and hummed a while longer then placed the tiny boy in his crib. This time he didn't stir. Standing above him, watching him sleep, a powerful love gripped Cassie.

When Austin returned ten minutes later, Cassie left her brother in charge of his wife and son and took her bowl of ice cream to her bedroom. She hadn't told Austin about the trip to Louis's trailer. He wouldn't approve. He thought she should let go of the past and move on. Perhaps she would have if Heath hadn't come along. But Darrell had been an important part of her life and now their short life together stood in question. Before she could move forward, she needed to close the door on the past. She simply had to know if her love and life with Darrell had been real.

Setting the red ceramic bowl on her dresser, she thought of the old chest and the things she'd found at the tornado site. She was still puzzled as to Heath's reason for wanting the map and the lipstick lid, but she trusted him to return them. She felt good admitting that. She trusted Heath. Trusted him with Darrell's belongings, trusted him to do the right thing. Maybe she even trusted him with her heart.

She paused to examine the notion. Found it good and

right and tucked it away inside. Someday soon, she would be ready, though she could scarcely believe a man like Heath would want her for anything more than a pal. But he did. Every action seemed to court her, to woo her, to draw her to him.

She'd had little time to look through the items she'd found this afternoon, but now she could. She spread the handful of documents on her bed, driven by a bittersweet eagerness to sort through them. One at time she opened the envelopes, read the enclosures. Mostly they included the normal, everyday bills of living with several pieces of advertisement, as if someone, probably Darrell, had tossed random mail into the drawer for later perusal. A glossy brochure for scuba equipment and reef diving. Another for condos on the beach. Another for Buenos Aires. The latter made her frown. Darrell had never mentioned Buenos Aires.

"Meet Dias. Cavern 2. 8." She read aloud from a slip of paper stuck inside one of their honeymoon brochures.

Cassie frowned at the words, pulse tripping in her throat. The writing was Darrell's. But who was Dias? She put aside the note to rifle through the others in hopes of a clue. She came across a reminder to rent a boat at a certain place and another with directions to a dive shop. The latter notation soothed her. Dias was likely another scuba enthusiast Darrell wanted to connect with in Mexico. No big deal. Nothing nefarious. No need to tell Heath.

Or should she? Weren't these items more proof that her honeymoon was exactly as it should have been?

A little voice niggled at her brain. *What if they're something else?*

They weren't. That's all there was to it.

She should tell Heath. Show him.

The photos of crystal white sand and impossible blues

of the Mexican seas gleamed under the overhead light like a beacon pointing the way.

For a long time, she sifted through the mementos, regretting without grief, mulling without resolution. Then, she slid them into a drawer beneath a stack of colorful scarves, and left them there.

"There you are, you lazy Fed. Where have you been?"

Heath had just ambled into the police station, past Verletta at the dispatch desk, past the administrative assistant who made both his and the chief's life easier, and into the cluttered office of his boss.

"It's six in the morning, Chief. I've been asleep for the last six hours." More like four, but who was counting? Last night, he'd been restless enough to clean his apartment and shoot a few emails to his brothers and mom. He'd even done some research on Mexican drug trafficking routes. Imagine that. The map he'd gotten from Cassie had rung a bell. He hadn't completely connected the dots to Darrell Chapman, but he had a good start now that he'd seen the map. "What's up?"

JoEtta shoved a cup of black coffee into his hands. "Had a call this morning. Some bigwig in another time zone without sense enough to look at the clock."

"Must have been a Fed," Heath drawled. Then he sipped the scalding brew, grimaced, and went back for another sip.

The chief smirked. "How did you know?"

He hoisted the coffee in a salute. She'd given him the mug with the "I see guilty people" logo. "Saw that dig coming. Who called?"

"Somebody trying to lure you away from Whisper Falls. Asked permission to contact you. As if my disapproval would stop him." She yanked another mug from the single shelf beneath the coffee cart.

"Why, Chief," he said, in the slowest Texas drawl he could muster. "I'm starting to think you like having my sorry federal agent hide hanging around."

She sniffed, shot him a narrow glare. "Don't break your arm patting yourself on the back. You're helpful at times. When you're not lollygagging over that hairstylist."

Heath's smile tightened. That hairdresser *was* taking a lot of his time. If not for the troubling matter of her late husband…"

"Well?" Chief demanded, a hand on her hip showing her typical impatience.

Heath flinched. He'd been thinking of Cassie again and had lost the train of conversation. As cover, he took another sip of coffee. The chief could sear the hair off a bald eagle with this stuff. "Well, what?"

"Do you, or do you not, want to talk to that bigwig Fed?"

"No need."

"No? Not interested in hogging all the glory anymore?" The constant jabs at his former DEA status didn't bother Heath. The chief knew the truth. She'd bowed to his knowledge and asked for his take on situations a number of times. She respected who he was. Correction, who he'd been. The joking around was just the way they related.

"Citations for extreme bravery clutter up my walls. Fame and fortune fades." He gave her an ornery grin. "Besides, somebody's got to keep these backwoods police chiefs in line."

JoEtta guffawed, jostling coffee onto the floor. She rubbed at the splatters with her boot toe. "So, you like us here in Whisper Falls, do you?"

"Something like that." He did. That much was true. Yet he remained troubled by the vow to his father's memory, worried he wasn't doing enough. Small town life was sweet, but it didn't offer many opportunities to bag the really bad guys. All the more reason to push harder on the Carmichael case.

"Don't tell me you haven't thought about going back to the agency." Flexibility had been part of their deal, a six-month trial period for both parties.

"Oh, I've thought about it." He took a chair, studied his coffee. "There are...situations." And he wasn't sure if the situations kept him here or gave him reasons to leave.

Chief Farnsworth circled the desk and plopped down, equipment and chair rollers clanking. "Cassie Blackwell?"

Feeling the acid burn in his gut, Heath set the coffee atop a file cabinet. He'd never even come close to having an ulcer. No use starting now.

He drew in a slow breath and let it out every bit as slowly. "Yes. Cassie."

The chief tilted back in her chair, crafty eyes studying him for two beats. "She doesn't have anything to do with this drug business, Heath."

The chief never used his given name. It made him feel young, vulnerable. He much preferred her bluster.

"Maybe. I hope not. She seems like a nice girl." *Nice girl. Yeah. Sure. Congratulations, Monroe, you slid that one out as if Cassie was nothing more than an acquaintance on the street. As if you didn't have crazy thoughts about her. Talk about compromised.*

"But you'll keep digging."

"Have to." He turned to retrieve his coffee.

"Your daddy was a good cop, too."

The statement turned him around, frowning. Had they discussed his father?

"Mace Walters told me." Those shrewd eyes narrowed, seeing more than he liked to show.

"Mace talks too much." Mace. Old friend and easy reference. But no use getting riled. His father's career was public record. Anyone could do an internet search and find the information in a matter of minutes. Heath sipped at his coffee, hiding the turmoil that spewed to the surface at the mention of his father.

"I needed to know who I was hiring. A family of law dogs, so to speak. Commendable. None of my brats followed in my renowned footsteps."

He could see that bothered her but knew better than to commiserate. She'd spit in his eye. He also knew she'd thrown in the latter intentionally, a way of showing him that she, too, had a cross to bear.

"Dad died in the line of duty, a drug raid gone bad."

Lips tight, she nodded. "A sorry shame, too. So you became a DEA agent."

"Somebody's got to do it." He gave up on the coffee and set the mug aside for good. "But today I'm satisfied to be Whisper Falls's assistant chief."

"Sure about that? You're seeing an awful lot of Cassie lately. What if the investigation into her husband goes south on you? How will you feel about Whisper Falls if that happens?"

"It already has gone south. All the way to Mexico."

But the chief already knew that, just as she knew he'd hired Holt to dig around across the border. "I could take over from here. Call in the city boys. Leave you out of the equation."

He was touched. In her inimitable manner, JoEtta was offering him a way out of the sticky situation.

"Too late, Chief. Cassie knows I started this investigation. Now, I have to finish it."

Chapter Twelve

A storm was brewing. Another of the Ozarks' magnificent displays of terrible beauty and supreme power. Like God, Cassie thought as she darted out the back door of the salon and through the fat splattering drops of rain. Laughing, she leaped through the SUV door held open by Heath Monroe.

The inside of his vehicle was redolent of Drakkar Noir, the scent clips in his air conditioner. The fragrance, combined with rain, reminded her of the stormy night they'd met.

"You should try out for the Olympics. Great sprint." He grinned at her as she settled in, hooked her seat belt and pushed damp hair from her eyes.

"Yes, and in heels." She lifted a foot toward him. "First place in ninth-grade track. 50-meter dash."

"In those shoes? Impressive."

Cassie snorted a laugh. The crazy sense of humor was one of the things she liked most about Heath.

A stray lock of damp hair stuck to her cheek. Heath noticed and looped it behind her ear. With a wink, he said, "Missed one."

Cassie's belly jittered. A silly reaction, she thought, but the brush of his fingers against her cheek set off romantic fireworks inside of her. She was tempted to lean over the console and kiss him hello, right on that cute chin patch. Maybe even above. She refrained, of course. She didn't want him getting the wrong idea, although at this point in their relationship she couldn't say what that was. She liked him. He liked her. They enjoyed spending time together. Just as she had done with Rusty. No, not true. Being with Heath was different, and she was wise enough to admit it.

"I'm not sure house hunting tonight is such a great idea," she said when the wayward thoughts subsided. "Tracking mud and rain into someone's rental won't make a great impression."

Considering, he sat with one arm over the steering wheel, his body shifted slightly toward her. She liked the way he could appear intense and relaxed at the same time. Focused, confident, but natural. As a special agent, she supposed he'd always been on guard.

"We can try another day," he said. "Are you still game for dinner or want me to take you back to your car?"

They'd met in the parking lot next to the salon. No point in going home only to have Heath drive all the way out to the ranch.

"And give up chili dogs and cheese fries? No way!"

"Compromise, then. My weather app says we're in for a nasty night. Let's skip house hunting and go straight for the junk food."

"I love the way you think." Oh, yes. She could love a lot of things about Heath Monroe.

"It's the training." He tapped his temple. "Astute mind. Keen senses. Always ready."

"For chili dogs?"

"Always."

They both laughed, and Cassie leaned back against the plush leather and relaxed. Today had been trying at the shop. A customer wasn't happy with a color and demanded a free redo, though both Cassie and Louise had warned her the new color wouldn't work with her skin. Then Michelle Jessup had come in and shot daggers and snide remarks toward Cassie, making the other customers uncomfortable. Then there was the matter of the mementos she hadn't mentioned to Heath.

Heath's tires splashed through puddles on the way to Johnson's Drive-In, the only fast-food joint in Whisper Falls. At least at the moment. Miss Evelyn was making noises about letting in a burger franchise, though many of the town's businesspeople, Cassie included, wanted to keep Whisper Falls more personal with local merchants only.

On the drive to Johnson's, Cassie talked nonstop about the day's events, especially the irritation with a jealous Michelle—which made Heath laugh, the rat. When she finally ran dry, she pried into his workday.

"Slow," was all he said. He was about as forthcoming as her brother.

Exasperated, she said, "You had to do something besides sit around and look cute."

"Except for the fender benders, rain keeps everyone pretty low-key." He pulled under the awning at Johnson's and left the motor running as he shifted in her direction. "Was that a compliment?"

She just smiled. Of course she thought he was cute. *Gorgeous* was a better word. She wasn't blind. "Order the chili dogs before I starve."

He rolled down his window, pushed the button and in minutes a carhop delivered chili-scented paper bags. When the girl left, Heath asked, "Eat here or my place?"

"Are you going to show me your etchings?"

"I would if I knew what they were, but since I don't,

how about if we kick back and watch something exciting? Like the weather."

"You're a wild man." Her stomach growled, making them both snicker. "Let's go before I pass out."

"I know CPR." His tone and expression were deadpan, but she saw the twinkle in those emerald eyes.

She gave him a mock glare. "Drive, Monroe, drive."

With rain drowning the windshield and warm, moist heat fogging the glass, Heath drove the few blocks through a quiet residential area to his apartment.

Like two escapees from Looney Tunes, they dashed from the car to the house, laughing through the downpour. Cassie squealed more than laughed. The rain was cold!

Dancing on one foot and then the other, she waited in the rain while Heath fumbled with the key and unlocked the door. She rushed inside and stopped on a furry brown rug. "I'll drip on your carpet."

"Let me get you a towel. Hang on."

While he was gone, she slipped off her shoes and looked around. An efficiency apartment, the living room bled into the dining-kitchen. Apparently a bed and bath was off to the left, though from here she couldn't see anything except a doorway. The small living space was tidy other than the scatter of mail on the coffee table and a shirt hanging over the back of an ordinary brown recliner.

She trailed her fingers over the shirt. He'd worn this one yesterday. An olive-green that accented his eyes and darkened his thick eyelashes.

"I haven't had a chance to do much to the place," Heath said as he returned and handed her a fluffy towel.

Cassie stepped away from the chair, hoping he hadn't seen her touching his shirt. What was wrong with her to do such a thing? Oh, but she knew. She was almost certain she knew.

The truth was, she was making excuses to be with him. Any excuse. House hunting, the weather, chili dogs, whatever it took. With Heath, her world brightened and centered. She hadn't felt centered in a long time. Maybe never. It was scary, too, to contemplate letting her heart go again, but she was afraid it might be too late to stop.

Yet his investigation of Darrell was like a sticker in the sole of her foot, and one she couldn't remove. Heath was an honorable man with a job to do. She couldn't ask less of him than to do his best. But her heart was caught somewhere in the middle.

"Thanks." She blotted her face and arms and dabbed at her skirt and hair. "I'm damp but not too drippy." She shivered.

"Are you cold? I could lend you a shirt."

That was way too tempting. "I'm good. Thanks. Did the chili dogs survive the mad dash?"

"Only one way to find out." He grabbed the brown bag and headed toward the table, a round, black pedestal style with two lattice-backed chairs, small and cozy. "Do we need plates?"

"Nope. I believe in avoiding dishwashing if at all possible." She opened his cabinets as if she belonged there and found two glasses. "Water?"

"Cokes in the fridge if you want one. Or if you're cold, I can make coffee."

"Water's fine with me. Maybe coffee later."

"Great. Let's chow."

He pulled out a chair and waited until she was seated. Did he have any idea how endearing that was? Of course he did. Heath Monroe was no dummy. He knew how to please a woman, and it pleased her to know he wanted to.

"I like the way you do that. Your mama taught you very nice manners."

"My dad was a gentleman. I remember that much clearly." He took the chair opposite her, making barely a scrape as he scooted in. "Mom insisted we boys follow his example."

She slid the hot dog boat from the waxy wrapper and leaned down for a whiff of spice. "Man, I love that smell."

"Taste is even better." He chomped a bite of his. She watched him, liked the way he chewed with complete masculine abandon.

"Tell me more about your dad. He sounds like a great guy."

"He was. The best dad, the best cop."

"You were how old?"

"Twelve."

"You probably have a lot of good memories."

"Yeah. Never enough, of course. My brothers were younger than me, eight and ten, so their memories are fewer. I'm sorry about that. Dad was an amazing man. Mom says I remember him bigger than life. She's probably right."

"Tell me something you remember about him."

"You don't want to get me talking about Dad. I could go on all night."

"Yes, I do. Please."

He set his chili dog on the table and pinched up a fry, pointing it at her. "Picture this. Houston in August, over a hundred degrees and so humid the air felt like soup. Dad came home from work. He had to be tired, but he'd bought us boys a Slip 'n Slide. Remember those?"

She nodded, but said nothing, letting him talk, enjoying the manly rumble of his voice, the easy drawl of south Texas.

"Instead of leaving us boys to play by ourselves, he played with us. He even sweet-talked Mom into playing, too. There we were, all five of us, screaming, laughing, soaking wet. Muddy and grassy, too, because we could never manage to stay on the slide." A smile tipped the corners of his mouth. "We played until dark that night."

Cassie smiled a little, too, touched that such a simple event lingered in his mind. Love and time and family all rolled together had that power. "It's a good memory."

"I don't know why that stands out, other than the fact that Dad was my hero." He scarfed another bite of chili dog, his eyes happy as he chewed and swallowed. "I saw him save a boy's life one spring. I must have been about ten at the time. Houston's prone to floods—you probably know that—and it had rained for days. The storm drains ran full and rapid the way they do after a big rain. A neighbor kid and I were playing, goofing off, being dumb, when he decided to take a swim in the flooded ditch."

"Oh, no."

"Yeah. One minute he was standing on the bank and the next he was gone. The current whipped him downstream that fast. I ran home to Dad, scared witless. I'll never forget his reaction. He went to one knee, grabbed me by the shoulder. Like this." His spread fingers pinched his left shoulder. "My legs were shaking, but all of a sudden I knew everything would be all right. Dad would take care of it." Heath dropped his hand to the table. "He told Mom to call 911. Then he grabbed a rope from the garage and ran."

"You followed him?"

"I had to. Bret was my pal. I felt responsible."

Responsible. She could see that. The boy had followed the man to adulthood. "How did your dad get him out?"

"He jumped in." Heath shook his head. "Every bit of training warns against it, but he couldn't reach Bret, not even with a long limb."

"That was incredibly brave."

"That was my dad. He tied the rope around his waist and had me tie the other end to the closest tree, a skinny thing I was afraid would snap under the strain. I think that's the first time in my life I prayed out loud."

"Was the kid okay?"

"Yes. Thank God. By the time rescue arrived, Dad had him out of the ditch." He huffed softly. "Bret never wanted to play in water much after that."

"Your dad saved his life."

"I'd always thought of my father as a hero, but that day, everyone in the neighborhood recognized it, too."

"If the situation arose, you'd do the same thing."

He twitched one shoulder. "I like to think I would."

He would. She knew it as surely as she knew this chili dog was spicy and warm. She took another bite, savoring the thick chili and the cheesy fries. Heath quickly dispatched his food and reached for one of her French fries.

"You steal my fries, you'll owe me."

He snatched the potato and popped it into his mouth. "Name your price."

"Oooh, that's a dangerous offer, Mr. Assistant Chief." She nibbled the end of a fry, pretending to contemplate. "Let's see. I could ask for the Taj Mahal. Or the crown jewels of Britain. But instead, I think you should make dessert." She popped in the fry.

"You think I can't cook."

"It might have crossed my mind."

"Then you, Miss Hair Salon Entrepreneur, would be wrong. I make great brownies."

"Now it's my turn to be impressed. A man who can cook."

"I bought a mix." When she lifted an eyebrow, he shrugged. "I like brownies. Mom showed me how to fancy them up. They're awesome."

Cassie shoved the remaining bite of chili dog into her mouth and rose from the table. "Come on, then, show me your stuff."

The next ten minutes were pure fun. While rain pattered against the roof, inside the cozy apartment Cassie and Heath made brownies. They bumped hips, snitched dabs of batter with their fingers and flirted outrageously. Cassie couldn't remember anything being as much fun in a long while. Which told how pitiful her frozen life had been.

"Chocolate chips? That's the secret?" she asked, snitching one to sample, when he dumped a quarter cupful into the batter.

"One of the secrets. More to come after they're baked."

Cassie watched in fascination—and more than a little attraction—as the strong cop whipped up the brownies and stuck them in the oven. Once the timer was set, Heath grabbed the partial bag of chocolate chips and led the way into the living room.

"Man, listen to that rain." The spring and early summer had been turbulent and didn't appear to be letting up.

"The rain doesn't worry me. Listen to that thunder." Heath fished out his cell phone and studied the screen. "Severe thunderstorm."

"Are we under a tornado watch?"

Cassie crossed to the window and opened the drapes. With the living room light behind her, she could see little more than the silvery puddles beneath the street lamp. She reached for the switch and turned off the overhead, plunging the living room into shadows and highlighting the storm outside.

"Doesn't look that way." He moved next to her so that they were both peering outside, faces close to the pane. Their breath made circular fog on the chilled window.

"I guess I'm weird, but I like thunderstorms if there's no threat of tornadoes," Cassie said.

"Yeah?" He swiveled his head toward her. "Me, too."

Thunder rattled the windows. Cassie jumped.

Heath's hand touched her waist, steadied her. "Easy."

Before she could think up a reason why she shouldn't, Cassie leaned into him, let her head rest against his shoulder. He responded by pulling her against his chest, her back to his front, cuddling her, his arms draped loosely around her waist, his breath soft in her ear.

"You smell good," he said. "This is nice."

Nice didn't begin to cover the tide of emotion. Though a storm raged outside and the trees whipped and swayed, Cassie felt safe and secure in the cradle of Heath's arms.

"I smell brownies," she said, mostly to calm her raging pulse.

He nuzzled the back of her neck and gave a small laugh. "A man's dream scents. Pretty woman and brownies."

She shivered. Goose bumps formed. She liked the tickle of his whiskers against her skin. "Don't forget chili dogs and pizza."

"Hmm. Those, too." He nibbled her earlobe. "Delicious."

Cassie closed her eyes, enjoying the moment. He rocked her side to side, his chin atop her head. In silence, they watched the storm and snuggled. No more, no less, but altogether romantic.

Pea-size hail pinged the grass, bounced off the driveway. Thunder rolled and echoed like kettle drums in a long, wide canyon.

"Someday let's watch a storm from above Whisper Falls," he said.

"I'd love that. Someday." The word tormented her. Would there be a someday with Heath Monroe? Did she want there to be? The answer was yes and it scared her.

With Darrell, falling in love had been easy and uncomplicated. Not with Heath.

He sighed, a heavy gust that let her know he was thinking heavy thoughts. His heartbeat, strong against her back, increased.

"What are you thinking about?"

"You," he said.

She didn't know where to go with that so she remained quiet, but her heartbeat also responded, thumping harder against her ribs.

His lips touched the hair above her ear. In a soft murmur, a whisper really, he said, "Something good is happening between us, Cassie. Do you feel it, too?"

She nodded, tightened her fingers against his. "Yes."

She felt it, but was it the right thing for either of them?

"Good," he said, "because I don't play games. You may as well know. I'm falling in love with you."

More powerful than nature's storm, the words shook her, thrilled her, sent her soaring. Hadn't they been moving toward this moment for weeks? Every time they were together, they'd gotten closer.

But he was Darrell's accuser. How could she let herself love him?

Yet she did. The strength of that emotion, growing deeper every day, rocked her world, thawed a frozen heart, filled the empty places within.

"Oh, Heath," she managed with a troubled sigh.

He must have recognized the confusion in the sound, for he slowly turned her body until they were facing. There, in the pale shadows, he cupped her face. "What is it? I moved too fast? You don't feel the same?"

A surprising clot of tears thickened her throat. "But I do."

"You do?"

Torn between wanting to throw her arms around him and the truth of who he was and what he believed, Cassie nodded.

He gathered her up close, his gorgeous face relieved and pleased. "I thought you were going to show me the door."

"Can't," she whispered, flirting. "It's your house."

"True." He bent his head and kissed her.

Thunder rumbled. Lightning flashed. A storm raged, both outside and in.

She was falling in love with the man who thought her late husband was a criminal. Even as she reveled in his embrace, Cassie's head whirled with guilt.

What about his investigation? What about the papers she was afraid to show him? How would they ever move forward with this between them?

Chapter Thirteen

It was after midnight when the storm subsided and conditions were safe enough for Cassie to go home. Heath followed her halfway, just to be sure she was okay and because he wasn't quite ready to let her go. They stopped on a country road, and he kissed her in the rain. They both chuckled as water dripped down their faces and into their mouths. She tasted cool as the rain, warm as the brownies they'd shared, and Heath had never experienced a more romantic moment. He loved her. He *loved* her. He couldn't quite take in the revelation, something he'd never expected to happen, something he'd never wanted.

But now he did.

Tonight had been special. He'd not intended to say the words. Not yet. But they'd popped out like uncovered popcorn too full of fire and energy to keep them in. Blame the storm. Blame the night. Blame the chili dogs.

Man, he felt good.

Back at his apartment, Heath collapsed on the bed fully dressed and stacked his hands behind his head to assess the situation.

At his choice of words, he grinned into the darkness.

Assess the situation. Even in love, he couldn't stop thinking like a special agent.

Cassie had liked his brownies with the melted chocolate chip and marshmallow topping. She'd even fed him a few gooey bites that forced him to touch his tongue to her skin. Bothered no small amount, he'd put a stop to that by nipping the end of her finger and making her laugh. Oh, he'd liked the feel of her fingers against his mouth. Too much. So he'd backed away to keep from reacting like a caveman.

He glanced at the clock. He really should get some sleep, but energy buzzed through him with the force of a hornet swarm.

Maybe they should have discussed the investigation into her late husband's ventures. And maybe he should have kept his emotions to himself until he'd cleared Cassie from suspicion—until he knew the truth about Darrell Chapman.

He tossed onto his side, tormented. He loved her. He believed her. But an experienced agent shouldn't. Not until the evidence cleared her.

Even if it did, and he prayed it would, how would she feel if he found her husband guilty?

Restless, his sweet evening spoiled by intruding thoughts, he took Dad's badge from the nightstand and held it while he prayed.

He'd done a lot of that lately. Praying—pleading—for a happy resolution to the case.

He must have fallen asleep because he woke to the sound of his cell phone vibrating against the wooden nightstand. He rolled toward it, felt the jab of Dad's badge against his side.

"Hullo." He cleared his throat.

"Hey, big brother. Were you asleep?"

Heath growled low in his throat. "Jerk."

The reaction delighted Holt. "Wake up. It's nearly 4:00 a.m., you sluggard."

Heath scrubbed a hand over his face, groggy and not a little grumpy. "You pull the wings off butterflies, too, don't you?"

"Stop grousing. I have an update for you on that Mexico drug operation."

Heath came fully awake, dropped his feet to the floor and clicked on the lamp. "Let me find a pen. I want notes."

"Too rum-dum to remember?"

Heath didn't bother to answer. His brother had a predilection for very early mornings and took mischievous delight in tormenting those who didn't. Heath put the phone down while he yanked open the small drawer in the bedside table and rummaged around, coming out with pad and pencil.

"All right," he said. "Whatcha got?"

"Enough, and more on the way, I hope. I'm still poking around but this should get your juices running. Louis Carmichael was a small-time dealer who wanted to play with the big dogs. He'd made two trips to Mexico by himself the year before sending Darrell."

"So Darrell was his mule." Heath's heart sank. Instinct had warned him. He'd hoped it was wrong.

"Looks that way. I have some other feelers out, some people I'm trying to find, but everything points in that direction."

"What about Carmichael? Any news on where he's hiding?"

"None. No sign of him here in this part of Mexico. Chances are he's in the States, laying low."

"Or dead like his cousin."

"A distinct possibility. If the two cousins decided to play games with the cartel, they were bound to lose."

"If he's alive, we need to find him. I want to know what he knows."

"I'm on it, Heath. Got some people digging in the human garbage dumps. We'll find him."

"Anything on Darrell's death? Was it an accident?"

"I have it from a pretty good informant that it was a take-out. And I ain't talking about Chinese food."

"Man." Heath grabbed the top of his hair and squeezed. "Then the honeymoon was a setup, an intentional trip to traffic drugs?"

"According to this same informant—who wasn't cheap, by the way—people are terrified of the cartel down here. Darrell was supposed to meet with a guy named Alejandro to make a money transfer. Nobody seems to know if that meeting occurred or not."

"But our boy Darrell turns up dead on the beach."

"Yes. Still in scuba gear."

"Why didn't they dump him at sea?"

"That would rouse too many questions, bro. If a scuba diving tourist has an accident, that's easy to explain. The official police report claims he dived too deep, got narced on nitrogen, drowned high and happy and washed ashore with the tide."

"Rapture of the deep." Heath understood the diving term. Nitrogen narcosis from diving too deep too fast could cause a diver to act irrationally, even to become intoxicated to the point he removed his regulator and drowned. "I don't believe it. Someone yanked his regulator or held him under."

"Most likely. But the other makes a great story to tell the grieving widow and the good old U.S. of A."

A deep groan escaped Heath at the mention of Darrell's widow. How would he tell her that Darrell was likely murdered in a drug deal gone bad? A drug deal her husband was directly involved in?

"Any indication that the widow was involved?" He held his breath and prayed.

"None. Can't completely rule her out, but the informant was surprised to hear she was in Mexico. Didn't know Darrell was married. Another says he didn't want her to know about the drug operation. If Chapman used the honeymoon as a cover—and I think he did—your girl Cassie was almost certainly an innocent victim."

Relief shifted through Heath. Cassie was innocent. Thank God. At least this was positive news.

"You still have the hots for her?"

Heath let a beat go by. Hots? He wished it was that simple. Hots went away with distance and time. What he felt for Cassie wouldn't go anywhere. "I'm falling for her, Holt."

"No way. Hard-hearted Heath falling in love? The straight arrow agent losing his heart to a suspect?"

"Knock it off."

Another hum of silence before Holt spoke again. This time his tone was understanding. "This is serious, isn't it?"

"Yeah. I think so."

"About time."

"You don't get it, do you, Holt? I'm about to implicate her husband in the international drug trade. Do you think she's going to throw herself into my arms and declare undying love when she hears that news?"

"I hear you. Sorry, bro." The brotherly commiseration helped a little. "What are you going to do?"

"What I have to do." What he always did. He grappled for Dad's badge and ran his fingers over the raised words. "My job."

After sharing with Holt the data he'd found on the map,

Heath pushed the end button and headed for the shower and the longest workday in recent memory.

All day, Heath was in the worst mood of his life and pretty much everyone in his wake knew it, particularly the two juvies he'd caught destroying public property. Grimly, he figured they'd never do that again.

Cassie had phoned at noon, asking to meet at Evie's for lunch but he'd used work as an excuse. He wasn't ready to face her, especially in a public place. As much as he hoped Holt could come up with more information, the evidence was already strong enough to turn over to his pals in the DEA.

By seven o'clock his excuses were gone. He got in the Expedition and pointed it toward Whisper Falls and the Blackwell Ranch.

Cassie touched her bare toe to the porch and set the swing in motion. The cool wood felt good against her feet, achy after a day of standing in heels. Austin called her crazy for wearing them but trendy shoes made her happy, confident. Foot cramps were a small price to pay.

With crochet in hand, she listened to the domestic sounds inside the house. Austin banging pans in the kitchen as he helped with the dishes. Annalisa's happy voice sharing every moment of baby Levi's day as if he was the only baby who'd ever spit up half his milk or wet a diaper.

The sweetness of it brought a prickle of tears. Cassie dashed at them with her crochet—a stocking cap, one of many she'd agreed to make for the church's Siberian orphan project. Funny how she disliked cooking or cleaning but crochet was fun. Cooking had been fun, too. With Heath.

Hoss and Jet, Austin's ranch dogs, ambled up from somewhere, grinning. "What have you two been up to? You look guilty."

The dogs flopped at her feet so that with every swing, her toes grazed Jet's back. The graying black Lab groaned with pleasure at the contact.

Beyond the ranch, beyond the brilliant green pasture land dotted with black cows, the ancient mountains formed a purple fortress. Evening sun splintered through the trees, cast patches of gold against the green grass on the yard. Along the porch edge, a black-and-yellow bumblebee buzzed sentinel above a purple coneflower. Last night's storm had washed the air, leaving it sweet and piercing.

Last night. She sighed.

Last night with Heath had been beautiful. She'd never expected to feel this way again, to have hope for the future with such a fine man. Not that their relationship had gone that far, but he loved her. Hands resting on the soft black yarn, she closed her eyes, reveled in the feeling of being loved and let it fill her.

For better or worse, she should have trusted him with the papers she'd found at the trailer. For better or worse. Like the marriage vows she'd taken with Darrell.

Tomorrow. She'd take the papers into town tomorrow.

Satisfied with the decision, she picked up the needle and yarn and began to chain stitch. Both dogs lifted their heads and looked toward the road, a sign that company was coming.

When a big black SUV turned into the drive and headed her way, Hoss and Jet ambled off the porch, tails fanning the air. Happiness swamped Cassie. If she'd had a tail she would have wagged it, too.

Heath.

She put the yarn aside and tripped barefoot across the soft grass to greet him, smiling broadly as she went. As Heath stepped out of the Expedition, she tiptoed up and kissed him. For brief seconds, his hands came up to grip her arms and he held her to him. Then he stepped back and removed his sunglasses.

Cassie's welcoming glow slipped away. "Something's wrong."

He hooked his sunglasses in the neck of his shirt. "We need to talk. Alone. Can we walk?"

A warning bell went off in her head. The last time they'd walked the ranch, he'd accused Darrell of dealing drugs. "Is this about Darrell?"

His shoulders—those broad, strong, responsible shoulders—sagged. "Yes."

He didn't want to tell her but he would. As much as she wanted him to let it go, forget his suspicions, law enforcement was too deeply ingrained in his nature. "Let me get my shoes and tell Austin where I'm going."

She hurried into the house and when she returned, Heath leaned against the front of his vehicle, staring into the woods, jaw hard as the mountains. He'd replaced his sunglasses.

He pushed off the truck and fell into step with Cassie and the two dogs, saying nothing. Cassie's heart rose into her throat, thudded frantically there. She didn't want to have this conversation. Not after last night. Not now. Now that she loved him.

She reached out to the side, slid her hand into his, heard his slow exhale.

The dogs darted into the woods, noses down. Cassie and Heath walked a hundred yards before either spoke again.

"You may as well get it over with," she said. "What did you learn?"

"I never wanted to hurt you. I hope you believe that. I wanted to be wrong."

The sunny day dimmed, her heart chilled. "What are you saying?" She could see he struggled with whatever was on his mind, dreaded her reaction, and Lord help her, she couldn't promise him anything. "Tell me."

He looked off through the valley gouged deep by an ancient glacier. "I'm sorry, Cassie. I wish I didn't have to tell you this, but Darrell smuggled drugs and money in and out of Mexico for his cousin Louis. We don't know yet how long they'd been working together. At least three trips. Likely more."

She loosened her grip on his fingers, pulled away. "You're wrong. I told you that before. Maybe Louis did those things but not Darrell."

"There are witnesses, Cass, and evidence. That map you found with the notes and circles? Places he'd been? Most are common trafficking routes and the others are hot spots of drug use. We're checking them out, but I'm confident we'll discover either Darrell or Louis made drops and pickups at each of those destinations. Or planned to."

She was already shaking her head. "Those were places he'd scuba dived. He told me about them. Showed me pictures."

"I'd like to see those pictures if you don't mind."

"What if I do mind?" Her heart hammered in her throat as she thought of the documents in her bedroom. She'd wanted to believe they were innocent just as she'd wanted to believe Darrell was innocent.

Heath stopped in the trail near a lush tangle of blackberry vines and Indian Paintbrush. His expression looked as bereft as she felt. With hands out toward her, he said, "Don't do this, Cassie. Don't make this harder. The evidence is clear. He used diving as a cover for his business."

Her stomach rolled, cramped. She folded her arms over her middle. "Always?"

Heath's gaze skittered away. "We don't know."

He was holding something back, but she was afraid to

ask, afraid she didn't want to know. She'd been so sure Darrell was innocent. She'd trusted him. But she trusted Heath, too.

"You keep saying we. Who is we? You and Chief Farnsworth? Your friends in the DEA? Who are you getting this information from?"

"My brother, Holt, at the moment. I told you about him. He's a private investigator. A good one. He went down to Mexico."

Her gaze flew up to his, disbelieving. "At your request?"

"Yes. At my request."

He claimed to love her, but he'd sent someone to Mexico to destroy her memories. To break her heart.

"He found proof?"

"Witnesses. Strong evidence." He took both her hands and oh, how she wanted to erase this moment and return to last night. "Holt's work is solid, Cassie. He's not wrong about this. He has a few names and addresses, meeting places. And he's confident there's more to discover."

She tugged her hands away, crossed her arms over her chest and held on tightly lest she fly into a million pieces. She had names and places, too. Now she realized what they meant. Her husband had been a criminal.

"The lipstick lid I found," she started, suddenly too aware of how important every detail had become.

"No drug residue, if that's what you're asking, though I thought there might be."

"Drug dealers use women's cosmetics to smuggle drugs?"

"They use anything they think will work."

Anything? She steeled herself against the thought pushing at the back of her brain. As much as it hurt, she had to know. "Our honeymoon?"

Heath went still, wary. "What about it?"

"You know what I'm asking." The truth would make you free. Wasn't that what Heath liked to say? And what the Bible promised? Then why did she feel as if her world was falling apart? As if last night's storm had ripped away her shelter and destroyed her.

"Tell me, Heath."

He glanced away and then back to her, arms limp at his sides. She saw compassion in his expression and knew the answer before he spoke.

"A reliable informant claims Darrell was smuggling money on that trip. He apparently tried a double cross. We're unclear on the exact details, but the cartel frowns on that kind of thing. I'm really sorry, Cassie."

"They killed him?" Her voice trembled. She could barely whisper the words.

"We're almost certain."

Cassie closed her eyes against the regret in his, against the sharp pain that stabbed through the center of her soul. Her stomach cramped like a virus.

Oh, Darrell. I loved you. I believed in you. In us.

But Darrell had lied to her. Her marriage had been a sham, a cover for drug trafficking.

Grief and shame flooded her. She'd been a fool, a needy, lonely woman caught up in a whirlwind romance by a handsome, smiling drug dealer who'd used her to cover his crime. Had he ever loved her at all? Or had their quick marriage been more about his need to cover a crime than about his love for her?

When she opened her eyes Heath had stepped closer, his expression worried. She wanted to accuse him of lying, but why would he? Heath had no agenda other than truth. A truth he'd do anything to learn.

If she hadn't been reeling, wounded, devastated, she

would have pitied him. "Coming out here to tell me couldn't have been easy."

"No."

Last night he'd claimed to love her. And she loved him. Even now, with her past shattered at her feet like the storm-damaged trailer, she yearned toward Heath, wanted him to hold her as he'd done last night, to comfort her.

"Could I ask you one more thing?"

"What's that?"

"Was our relationship—you and me—" She started and stopped, floundering for the words, wanting reassurance while fearing the worst, her mouth dry as bleached bone. "Were you only with me because of this investigation? Is that why you asked me out?"

"No!" He spun away, spun back, face desolate. "At first."

"I see." The ache rose into her temples, pounding there with cruel efficiency. Two men she'd love. Two men had used her for their own means. Maybe she was the kind of woman no man could ever truly love.

"Cassie," he said. "It's not like you think. Let me explain."

"You lied to me."

"I didn't." He reached for her. "I was doing my job."

At what cost?

Palms pushed out, she resisted, shaking her head, frantic she'd burst into tears if he touched her. She bit down on the inside of her lip, holding on to her control. "Well, there you go, then. You've done your job. Now I think you should leave."

His arms fell to his sides, jade eyes searching hers. "Let me walk you back to the house."

"I'll be fine." She'd hurt and survived before. She could do it again. Oh, but this was different. This pain—double betrayal from the men she'd loved—ripped like a saw blade.

"I don't want to leave you—"

You already have. "Go, Heath. Please, do me that courtesy."

"We have to talk. I'll call you—"

"No. I need to be alone. I need time." Two lifetimes at least.

He fisted both hands on his hips, nostrils flaring. Emotion swam in his eyes. Confusion, anger, sorrow. "Is this what you want? The way you want it to end?"

Her head jerked up. "Nothing is the way I want, Heath. It simply is."

Before she could make a more complete fool of herself, Cassie turned her back, called her dogs and sprinted up Blackberry Mountain, leaving Heath Monroe behind.

Chapter Fourteen

For a solid week, Heath, aching and angry, used every spare moment to research the case of Darrell Chapman and Louis Carmichael, praying, hoping, dreaming that he'd find something better to share with Cassie. He'd broken her heart, watched her crumble before his very eyes and then walk away from their budding love.

She'd hated him for the truth. But he'd had no choice. Truth was truth.

Then why did he ache and yearn? Why did he lie awake at night longing for a way to make things right with her again?

Some part of him hoped to clear Darrell and play the hero, bringing Cassie good news instead of bad. Instead, the more he learned, the more convinced he became that two small-time operators had gotten in over their heads. If he could only find Carmichael for questioning, he'd be happy.

No, that wasn't true. He wouldn't be happy. He'd devastated the woman he loved and that was a hard pill to swallow. She'd broken him, too, the moment she'd turned her back and left him. He loved her. Wasn't that enough? But he knew the answer and it stung like a burn. She'd loved Darrell's memory more than a future with the agent who'd discovered the truth.

Still, he couldn't let go. He'd called her every day, not knowing what he'd say but needing to hear her voice. She refused to answer. Twice he'd seen her. In a small town like Whisper Falls, running into each other was inevitable, but she'd ignored him. Turned and walked the other way as if he was invisible.

There was no denying how much that hurt.

But his father's death had taught him that the price of justice was sometimes high.

As he turned the corner of Oak and Fairdale near the park, he spotted a car with a missing taillight and executed a traffic stop. He still felt strange performing routine police work such as this, but he pulled to the curb behind the car and scanned the Ford's interior before stepping out of his vehicle. Thinking tactically had saved his life on more than one occasion.

Fortunately, today he was in no danger. The taillight belonged to Haley Carter, Cassie's artist friend.

Allowing a smile, Heath approached the window Haley had rolled down. "Morning, Haley. Did you know you have a taillight out?"

The pretty auburn-haired woman turned her head toward the back as if she could see her fender. "Do I?"

"Yes, ma'am."

She screwed up her face in a grimace. "Does that mean I'm getting a ticket?"

"No ticket. Just get the light fixed. Wouldn't want an accident with that cutie in the back." He bent low to look in at Haley's little girl. "Somebody's catching a nap."

Haley laughed, a wind chime sound. "Anytime she's fussy, I take her for a ride."

"And that puts her out like a light?" The little one's head was flopped to one side, her bow mouth lax, long lashes stroking her pink cheeks.

"Every single time. Just wait. When you have kids, you'll do the same thing."

When he had kids. Like that was going to happen.

"Yeah," he said, but his heart wasn't in it.

"Listen," Haley said, squinting up into the sun. "I've been meaning to ask Cassie, but since you stopped me, I'll ask you. Creed and I would love it if you two would drop by for a visit sometime. We could have a cookout."

Heath was thankful for sunglasses.

"Appreciate the invitation." Not going to happen but it was nice of her to ask. He tapped the top of the car with the flat of his palm. "You get that taillight fixed today. Okay?"

"Promise. I'll run out to the heliport right now and have Creed do it."

"Sounds like a plan. You have a good day now."

"Don't forget to ask Cassie," she said right before her window closed.

Heath watched her pull away and then headed back to his truck, stomach churning. Friends considered Cassie and him a couple. So had he. But given his line of work, perhaps this way was better.

The fact that she didn't want to see him made sense. By doing his job, he'd hurt her and he hated that. He'd shattered her illusions about Darrell. He'd destroyed her fantasy of their perfect love, but knowing why she hated him didn't make it any easier to let her go. They were just beginning. Now they were done.

His radio crackled and he answered. "Monroe."

"Heath, Pudge has a problem down at the bait shop. A couple of rowdies trying to fight." There was nothing stiff or fancy about Whisper Falls dispatching. She simply stated what needed to be done.

"I'll head over there now."

"Oh, and Heath? That DEA guy called again. Says he wants to sweeten the pot, whatever that means."

"Got it. Thanks, Verletta."

In less than three minutes, Heath was inside the fishy-smelling bait shop and in five more, two men, both drunk, were handcuffed and in the backseat of his SUV. After booking them into the jail to sleep it off, he headed into his office to do the paperwork and make that call.

"Agent Jefferson. Heath Monroe."

"Monroe, good to hear from you." Heath's old boss had a voice straight off the streets of Philly where he'd grown up. "You know why I'm calling. Are you ready to come back to work for us yet?"

Heath rubbed at the whisker patch on his chin, contemplating. The timing was perfect. Maybe the phone call was God's way of nudging him along. "I've been thinking about it. What do you have in mind?"

The line buzz said he'd surprised Jefferson with the easy admission. But why not go back to a job he loved and was good at? Nothing for him here in Whisper Falls anymore.

"I've got a promotion with your name on it and a nice pay bump. I can also offer you a choice of location. How does that sound?"

"Sounds promising."

"Don't play with me, Monroe. Give it to me straight. You're one of my best agents. You don't belong in a tiny place like Whisper Falls. You've too much expertise and we need you. They don't."

His old boss was only partly right. Fancy lot of good his expertise had done him in Whisper Falls. The only time he'd used it, it had cost him the only woman who'd ever made him think about forever.

Heath kicked back in his roller chair and surveyed the small office he shared with the part-timers. His jacket hung on a peg. A photo of his nephews and niece was propped on his desk and a colored picture Ashley sent him was thumbtacked to the bulletin board. He'd started to settle in. "How soon do you need to know?"

"Today, tomorrow, next week. The sooner the better." Jefferson cleared his throat. "I'll start the paperwork." He chuckled. "You'll come back. It's in your blood."

After Heath rang off, he sat at his desk staring at a different kind of paperwork and thinking. Drug enforcement was his career, his life, his commitment to justice in memory of his father. As his former boss had reminded him, he was good at it.

He opened the photo gallery on his phone and scrolled through. Half the shots were of Cassie, of something they'd done, somewhere they'd been. Simple snapshots with her dogs, with baby Levi, with brownie batter on her nose.

A searing pain cut through him, hot and expanding inside his chest until he wondered if he'd erupt like a volcano. He loved her. But that was over. Her silence was signal enough, and belaboring the point would only hurt them both more.

He closed the app.

Whisper Falls was a fine town. He liked the people and if he were ever to settle anywhere permanently, Whisper Falls could be the place.

He pulled Dad's badge from his pocket and placed it on the desk, a reminder of his vow, of his calling. The war on drugs needed him more than Whisper Falls.

Cassie heard the rumor from Michelle Jessup who'd delivered the news like a cat with a belly full of cream. Heath was leaving. She'd been so shocked at the news she'd spilled a bottle of shampoo in Mable Harmon's lap and all over the floor. Cleaning up had taken forever and Michelle had sauntered out of the salon as pleased as could be.

Cassie supposed she shouldn't be surprised that a man of Heath's background and training would grow bored with the slow, small-town pace. Still, some foolish, broken part of her yearned to see him. He didn't know, couldn't know that she watched the street for his black Expedition and ached each time he parked in front of Evie's Sweets and Eats. She was being ridiculous, all things considered. They were as over as last year's replacement TV shows.

"Earth to Cassie. Earth to Cassie. I'm busy over here." Louise raised a bottle of nail polish above the hands of a customer. "Answer that phone, please."

"Oh. Sorry." Cassie grabbed for the landline. "Tress and Tan Salon. Cassie speaking."

With the receiver cradled between her neck and shoulder, she went through the motions of handling the caller, though her heart wasn't in the conversation. Her heart wasn't in much of anything these days.

She hung up the phone and finished folding a load of clean-scented towels while Louise completed Betsy Loggins's manicure. When the woman left and the shop was empty, Cassie's friend and partner stormed around her workstation.

"Want to talk about it? Or should I say him?"

"Nothing to talk about."

"Oh, please. Spare me. Think I don't know the signs? You've been distracted and quiet for a week. Heath doesn't come around anymore. You don't dance out the door to meet him at five every evening. You're not—" she threw her hands out to the sides "—sparkling."

"We broke it off." Cassie concentrated on making a perfect square of the hand towel.

"So what? Don't let a little spat and your silly pride stand in the way. Kiss and make up. You love him."

"Just leave it alone, Louise." Cassie turned away to put the stack of towels on a shelf. "I know you mean well, but Heath and I can't work out. He's leaving."

Louise marched around in front of her. "Who said?"

One hand trailing the terry towels, Cassie admitted, "Michelle popped in with the news this morning. You were over at Evie's chowing on cherry Danish."

"Michelle wants him. She lied to throw you off the scent. You should ask him yourself."

"Maybe I will." And maybe she was looking for another lame excuse to talk to him. Was she so pathetic that a man could betray her and she still wanted him? Her head was tangled with crazy thoughts and uncertainties. She didn't know anything anymore. "I think I'll take an early lunch. Carly canceled."

Louise slumped into a pitiful expression and whined, "Again? Her nails, too?"

"Sorry."

Louise rolled her kohl-rimmed eyes. "Nothing like waiting until the last minute."

"She always does." Grabbing her wallet, Cassie exited the shop and walked across to Evie's shop, eager to avoid more discussion of Heath Monroe. If he left town, she could forget him, and maybe he'd take his evidence and accusations with him and no one would ever know what a fool Cassie Blackwell had been.

Inside Evie's Sweets and Eats, she strode to the counter, pointy heels tip-tapping, to order a chicken salad wrap and baked chips. The place was busy, the few tables crammed with customers, so she had to wait. Normally, she'd use the time for conversation with other businesspeople and friends who frequented Evie's, but today she didn't feel like talking to anyone.

When her food came, she took the items and turned to leave, thinking a walk in the park might do her good. Before she reached the door, the knob turned and Heath stepped inside.

Heath looked up, saw Cassie standing inside the door and felt his world stop. He slowly removed his sunglasses, drinking her in like a man in a long drought. When he reached her eyes, his chest contracted. Escape was written all over her face.

Hurt, wary, unsmiling, he said, "Cassie."

"Heath."

She looked good. Beautiful.

As if they were both on freeze frame neither moved. Heath's pulse bounced against his collar.

"How are you?" he asked and then softer, "Are you okay?"

"I'm fine. Thank you." So stiff and formal, as if he'd never said "I love you." As if he hadn't held her and kissed her. "Yourself?"

He leaned closer, touched her elbow. "I tried to call you."

She edged her arm away, clenched it to her side. "I've been busy."

Too busy to care? Too busy to listen, to understand that he'd meant her no harm, but he'd had to do his job?

"I heard you might be leaving Whisper Falls."

His mouth went grim. A man had no privacy in this town. A decision not yet made and already the rumor mill had him gone. "Word gets around fast."

"So it's true?"

"I'm considering." *Unless you want me to stay.*

"Is it your old job? The DEA?"

"My boss called me again this morning."

"He must want you back badly."

He'd told her about the other calls but this one was different. "He offered a promotion, choice of locations, more money." Though Heath had never been about the money.

"Where will you go?"

"Wherever I choose." He told her the options, the job description, made the opportunity sound impressive mostly to convince himself that he wanted to travel again. But not to Mexico. Never again to Mexico.

When he finished the explanation, she beamed a bright smile that should have warmed him but left him cold instead. "You'll take it, then, and you'll be the best. The job sounds perfect for you."

"I suppose." *Will you miss me? Will you be sad I'm gone or will you sweep us away like castaway curls from your salon floor?*

His radio crackled. He wanted to rip the device from his belt and throw it out the door. "Excuse me while I check this call."

"I need to get back to the shop. Good luck on the new job."

"Cassie," he started and then didn't know what to say. He didn't want her to go. He wanted to tell her, but there was so much inside and all of it useless at this point. He was who he was. He couldn't change even if he wanted to. Full of regret and longing, he simply said, "Take care of yourself. Be happy. I want you to be happy."

Her bright smile wavered but she found it again.

"You, too. I mean that, Heath. I wish you every good thing. I'll pray for you." Her fingertips grazed his shirt sleeve. "I'll always pray for you."

Before he could delay her any longer, she slipped past him and out the door.

Cassie couldn't do this anymore. Her face was about to crack. She couldn't go on smiling and pretending all was well when she was crumbling inside.

Heath was leaving. Anything they might have had would go with him. Nothing she could say or do would stop him anyway. She was the gullible fool who'd married a drug dealer, and he was the DEA agent with the powerful sense of right and wrong. He must think she was stupidest woman on the planet, a woman whose new husband hadn't loved her enough to protect her from himself—if, indeed, Darrell had ever loved her at all.

For the rest of the afternoon she went through the motions of styling hair and friendly chitchat, none of which she remembered. All she could think of was the conversation with Heath. Like a revolving door, his words circled back again and again. He wanted her to be happy. How in the world did he think that was possible?

When the day finally ended, she got in her car and drove home to the ranch. Austin and Annalisa had taken the baby in for his checkup and hadn't yet returned, for which she was thankful. She didn't want to talk to another person. She didn't want anyone else to ask what was wrong.

Other than the faithful dogs, Cassie was blessedly alone. Restless, hurting, needing to think and pray, she changed clothes and saddled her horse for a long, private ride in the woods.

As the buckskin plodded up the trail, past the place where she'd learned the truth about her pseudo-marriage, the sun warmed her back and shone glossy on the horse's cream-colored neck. In the west, thunderheads built, huge and white and fluffy like a giant's cotton balls.

She passed a vivid orange butterfly weed, alive with thirsty monarchs. Black-eyed Susans lined the pathway, nodding their sunny faces toward her in greeting or perhaps in sympathy. June, the month of brides, was beautiful in the Ozarks. Normally, the natural beauty refreshed her. Today she simply prayed for peace.

Letting the horse take the lead, Cassie rode for a while without direction. When she heard the gush and roar of Whisper Falls, she realized this had been her destination all along.

She'd prayed here months ago to feel alive again. And look what that had brought her.

Dismounting, she tied the horse near a stand of grass at

the base of the pool and started the ascent to that secret, spiritual place behind the foaming cascade of water.

Spray coated the rocks and dampened her face and hands. She was halfway up when the tears came, hot against the cold spray. God had answered her original prayer. The numbness was gone. She could feel again, but she had discovered the hard way that feeling hurt too much.

Too burdened and heavy to continue, she abandoned the climb and came instead to sit on the gray limestone rocks beside the pool at the base of the waterfall. Lacy ferns formed a canopy overhead. Knees drawn up under her chin, Cassie stared into the mirrored pool and prayed. She prayed to understand God's will and direction. She prayed for Heath, for his job and his future wherever his pursuit of justice might take him because she loved him. Most of all she prayed for God to tell her where to go from here. She couldn't trust her own judgment about men, not after the double fiascos.

Losing Darrell had been sharp and cruel and fast. Losing Heath was a slow, burning agony.

She couldn't return to business as usual. For so long after Darrell's death, she'd convinced herself that she was destined to be alone, the sister, the friend, the best salon operator in the Ozarks. No matter how much she enjoyed her work and her brother's family, her life felt empty and meaningless without love. Not love for love's sake. Without Heath.

But Heath was leaving. For all his sweet words and passionate kisses, like Darrell, he hadn't loved her. He'd needed her for an investigation, and love had been his weapon.

At the harsh reality of that bitter, bitter truth, Cassie put her face on her knees and grieved.

Chapter Fifteen

Heath hadn't accumulated much in his short few months in Whisper Falls. As usual, moving on should be easy.

He perched his hands on his hips and surveyed the little apartment. Not much to pack. A few boxes. His clothes and personal effects. His computer and TV. A man couldn't get along without his big TV. All of his belongings would fit in the back of the SUV. One trip and he'd be gone for good, never to look back.

He sank into the old brown chair and rubbed his palms over his face. Who was he kidding? He'd be looking back at Whisper Falls for years, maybe forever. A man didn't fall in love every day of the week and then forget about it.

He thought about driving out to Cassie's house. Maybe if they talked one more time, maybe things would work out.

Heath chuffed, a sharp sound in the silent apartment. "Who are you kidding?"

Nothing could work out with Cassie. He'd blown that chance. Even if he could go back and change what happened, he wouldn't. Oh, he might handle a few things differently, but Chapman and Carmichael were dirty and deserved justice. That was the Monroe way and he was duty bound. He couldn't expect Cassie to understand. Nor could he expect her to forget that he was the man responsible for sullying her husband's name.

A knock sounded at his door. Heath spun toward the entry, hope leaping in his chest, powerful and out of control. "Cassie."

He flipped the locks and yanked the door inward.

A dark, lanky man leaned against the door frame, grinning his ornery grin.

"Holt?" The pulse in Heath's throat began to slow as hope turned to curiosity. "What are you doing here?"

"Can't a man visit his big brother?"

"I'll be in Houston next week. You could see me then. Is something wrong? Is Mom all right?"

"Relax. The family's fine." His brother pushed away from the door to look toward the distant landscape. "Always wanted to see an Ozark summer. I thought I'd take the scenic drive."

Granted, Whisper Falls was a spectacular jewel in summer with birds and butterflies, flowers and trees a riot of color and life, but he didn't believe Holt for a second. "If that's true, where are Krissy and the kids?"

"Dropped them off in Texarkana to see her folks. She sends her love."

"So you came alone."

"Yep."

A thought that had been circling around Heath's brain popped to the front. "Mom sent you."

Holt's slow, wide smile eased up his cheeks. "Looks like my cover's made, but don't be blaming Mom. We might have talked but I brought myself. You gonna let me in?"

"Oh, sure." Surprised at himself for keeping his brother at the door, Heath stood to the side and let him enter.

"Small but nice." Holt did a quick survey, his PI gaze missing nothing. "Great TV. You get cable up here?"

"Satellite."

"HD?"

Heath smirked. "This is the Ozarks, not Timbuktu."

Holt barked a laugh and slapped his hand atop the TV. "Man, it's good to see you."

"Same here." Heath couldn't help smiling at his younger sibling. As a kid Holt had been as hyper as a terrier. The man was full of focused energy. "You're looking tan."

"Mexican beaches are great. Especially on your money." Holt smirked, a brotherly gotcha as he circled the room in his long, loose stride. "You're already packing?"

"Collecting boxes. I'll pack next week. You want a Coke or something?"

"Thanks. I'm parched." Holt folded his long body into the brown recliner and accepted the Coke Heath offered. "What's the hurry? A few weeks ago, you were loving on this quiet Ozark outpost."

"Things change." Heath flopped onto the couch. He was glad to see his brother again whatever the reasons. Phone calls were great, but in person rocked the house. He missed his family.

"The Mexican problem have anything to do with this sudden change?"

Heath dragged in a breath, exhaling on a gusty sigh. "Yeah. It does."

"Figured as much. Mom said you were pretty messed up about something and being the brilliant strategic thinker I am, I put two and two together and came up with the widow you're in love with."

Heath sat upright. "I never said I was in love with her."

"Yes, you did. You are. For the first time I can remember, you talked about a woman the way I talked about Krissy before I let her snag me. The way I still do." Holt tilted his Coke can like a finger point. "Stop trying to blow smoke at a master investigator, and give it to me straight. What's going on down here? Why are you jumping ship? How does the widow fit into all this? I told you she was clean and getting cleaner with each piece of the puzzle. So what's the problem, bro? Grab your lady and do-si-do."

Heath leaned back against the couch and stared up at the ceiling fan stirring the air in lazy swipes. Holt would keep pecking at him until he knew everything just the way he kept pecking at an investigation until all the parts fell into place.

"All right, here's the deal." His shoulders slumped. He, a decisive, life-and-death kind of guy couldn't run his own business anymore. "I messed up. I started seeing Cassie—Darrell Chapman's widow—for the wrong reasons. Mostly."

"What exactly does that mean?"

"I took her out at first to discover what she knew about her husband's operation."

His brother made a humming sound. "Dude, you are in a world of hurt."

"Yeah, well, thanks. That helps a lot."

Holt lifted both palms. "Just saying."

"At the time I thought she might be implicated in the drug ring. I liked her, enjoyed her company, but in the beginning I was all about the investigation."

"You let her think it was more?"

"Basically."

"Oh, son." Holt dragged out the word with a shake of his head. "Bad move. You're lucky to still be breathing."

Holt didn't know Cassie. She didn't fight. She retreated. Fighting might have felt better. Clear the air, let it rip.

"My plan was fatally flawed from the beginning. Instead of thinking small town, I acted like an undercover agent. Infiltrate, get to know her, pry out some information and move on. A normal investigation, exactly the kind I've done for years."

"You dated suspects?"

"No, I didn't date suspects!" The idea made him mad. Did his brother really think he was that low? When it was necessary, he befriended suspects and got to know them. He didn't date them. "Never."

"Until now. Until Cassie." Holt hummed again, his restless foot making slow circles. "You may have thought you were out to collect evidence, but the heart knew something you didn't."

"Tell me about it. I was blindsided. One day, I'm praying she reveals something in the case and the next I'm praying she's innocent and wondering how to get out of this mess without breaking her heart or mine."

Holt was nodding, his sharp, analytical mind filling in the blanks. "Then I call from Mexico with a break in the case. As the case unravels so does your romance. You get the bad guys, you lose the girl."

"Something like that." Heath studied the side of his condensing Coke can, recalling the look of shock and betrayal on Cassie's face. "Cassie didn't take the news well."

"You told her? That you'd dated her as part of the investigation?"

"Unintentionally." When Holt only stared as if he thought his older brother was an idiot, Heath shrugged. "She asked."

"Then she threw you out."

"Basically." Threw him out, turned her back, handed him his heart on the side of a summer-blessed hill.

He took a long, burning pull on his Coke.

"So you decided to quit your job and hit the road again. Forget about the woman."

"The DEA is what I know. What I'm good at. I apparently don't do so well with small towns and personal relationships. What other choice did I have?"

"You can dig in your heels and make this thing work. Call the lady up. Go see her."

"Won't happen. She hates me, not only because I dated her for the wrong reasons but for proving her husband was a do-wrong. She thought he was a superhero, a Romeo who doted on her." Heath tapped his chest with one finger. "I'm the guy who shattered her fairy-tale illusions. You think she's going to forgive that?"

"Have you told her how you feel, and that you hate what happened? That you wish you could change it?"

"She knows."

"Does she? Let me give you a piece of advice, bro. Women need words." When Heath stared at him with hopeless eyes, Holt clumped the soda can on the coffee table. "You know what I think?"

"No," Heath answered wryly. "But I'm pretty sure you're going to tell me."

"And you'd be right." Holt sniffed. "You're afraid of commitment. You love this girl, and you're afraid."

A quick jolt of anger had Heath leaning forward, fists clenched. "Don't be a moron. My middle name is commitment. To justice. To the drug war. To Dad's memory. My record stands for commitment. You know that better than anyone."

A tiny smile tilted the corners of Holt's mouth. "Stirred you up a little, didn't I?"

"Yeah." More than a little.

His brother tilted back in a long, easy stretch and crossed his legs. Only his dark eyes, brown points of radar, revealed his intensity. No wonder Holt was a good PI. He'd come on affable and relaxed while prying every bit of information from a source. And then, bam! Like a mouse trap, he sprang.

"The family had a meeting, Heath."

"About me?" Heath touched a hand to his chest, surprised again. "A meeting?"

Holt nodded. "Heston and Mom wanted to come along on my little scenic drive. I told them I'd handle this first round. But if they need to come down and talk to you, I can give them a call."

"What is this? Some kind of intervention?" He felt a little horrified by the thought. He was the man of the family, not some troubled teen or struggling alcoholic.

"Take it how you want. We're worried. All your adult life, you've been married to your job, taking the worst assignments in the most dangerous, darkest places."

"Nothing wrong with that. Somebody's got to do it."

"Other agents get married, buy a house, settle down. Not you. You've never even owned a dog. Man, there is something sick about that."

"Lots of people don't own dogs."

"You like dogs. You're the kid who slept with a flea-bitten mutt until you left for college."

"Addie didn't have fleas."

"No, she had puppies and you wanted to keep them all."

True. He missed having a dog and had enjoyed hanging out with Cassie's friendly, furry trio. "Dogs need lots of attention. I wasn't around that much to take care of one."

"My point exactly. When you left the agency and moved to Whisper Falls, Mom was overjoyed. Finally, her eldest was growing roots. When she learned you were dating someone special—" Holt raised his hands in a hallelujah.

"Courtesy of my big-mouthed brother, I suppose."

"Of course." Holt showed his teeth. "Here's the deal in

a nutshell, Heath. You've allowed Dad's death to take over your life. It's time to let it go."

The statement rocked Heath. Let it go? Abandon his vow to honor his father in exchange for personal happiness? "I can't. Dad was my hero. He deserves justice."

"We've given him justice, Heath. All of us boys are doing our part to fight crime. All of us honor him every day of our lives. You're the only one who's taken the responsibility too far."

"Not possible."

"Yes, it is. Dad was first and foremost a family man. He loved us, Heath. He wanted the world for his boys and Mom."

"Yes." Heath rubbed a hand over his whiskers. "Yes, he did. He was the best."

"Do you think you're the only son who loved him that much?"

The question struck him in the chest like a bullet. "No, of course not."

"Do you think Heston and I don't do enough? That we don't do our part to honor Dad's memory and legacy?"

"I don't think that at all."

"Good, because I'd have to take you down and spit in your ear if you even suggested such a thing."

The silly statement lightened the mood. Heath grunted, remembering some of the ornery things brothers did to each other.

"Dad would be proud of you both."

"I believe he would. Being an honest member of law enforcement *and* a good family man is the way I honor our dad. Do you hear what I'm saying, Heath?"

"Maybe I do." Heath nodded, the light slowly dawning. "Yes, I think I do."

All these years he'd subjugated the personal side of his

life in pursuit of justice for his father. He'd believed with all his heart that Dad would have expected that much from the oldest son. But Holt was right. Dad wouldn't have wanted that. Dad was a man first, a cop second. Somewhere along the line, Heath had turned the priorities around.

"Tell me one thing, bro," Holt said softly. "Do you really want to leave Whisper Falls?"

"No." There was the truth. A truth that would, indeed, set him free. The weight he'd carried for weeks, perhaps years, lifted from his shoulders. "I was happy here until—"

Holt pushed up from the chair to clamp a long, hard hand on Heath's shoulder. With understanding in his voice, he said, "Maybe you should give that lady of yours a call."

Hope plummeted. Truth or not, Cassie and he were over. "She won't answer."

"Then go see her. Talk to her. Make her listen. At least try."

That faint hope glimmered back to life. He didn't know if Cassie would ever forgive him for being the man who used her to bring down her husband, but he was going to find out.

Bent over the changing table, Cassie fastened the tabs of Levi's tiny diaper. Fresh from his bath, the little man smelled sweet and clean and his translucent skin gleamed under the overhead light. Even after his scary start, her nephew was thriving enough that Austin and Annalisa had left him with Aunt Cassie to have their first date night since the birth.

"Aunt Cassie loves that idea," she said as she swaddled him in the soft, blue blanket and then picked him up. She inhaled the fragrance of him, thankful to God that he was healthy and strong. "You're a handsome boy. Just like your daddy. What?" She pretended to listen. "Oh, if you insist. I'll give your pretty mama some credit, too."

Tootsie, the poodle, lifted her head from the floor and cocked an ear.

Cassie grinned, both at the poodle and her own silliness. At only a few weeks old, Levi still looked more like a wrinkled old man than either of his parents, but someday, he'd be a lady-killer.

"You're going to be a gentleman, too. Not like some men I could name." Men who would lie and use women. Men who put their own agendas before the women they claimed to love.

The bitter root she'd been fighting dug a little deeper. She'd prayed for God to take away the anger and hurt, and she wanted to understand. She'd even talked to her close friend Haley about the situation. Sweet Haley had sympathized but advised her to look at things from Heath's point of view. Then she'd told her to get in there and fight for the man she loved.

"Heath's point of view? Really?" She had no idea what that was, but if he cared for her, he wouldn't be leaving town. He wouldn't have misled her.

And Cassie had no fight left in her.

Levi started to fuss and Cassie carried him to the rocker. With a toe to the floor, she set them in motion, snuggling the soft bundle to her chest. "Better to focus on you than men. Even if you will be a man someday."

As if he understood, Levi squinted midnight-blue eyes at her for a full five seconds before they crossed. Cassie smiled. He was so adorable, her nephew. She loved being an aunt, was thankful to have this opportunity to love a child. Grateful because she was done with men. Levi was as close as she'd get to having children. "So I'd better enjoy you, little mister." She kissed him on the tiny nose.

The house was quiet. No TV. No music player. Tootsie curled on the rug beside the changing table, chin on her paws, listening with drowsy eyes. Cassie enjoyed the house like this, when she could hear the air vibrate and the baby's breaths.

She rocked the infant, letting her mind drift to the pretty artwork on one wall—a night scene of the moon and stars above a silver lake lapping against an empty, peaceful shore. Though she didn't want to go there in her memories, she recalled the last full night of Darrell's life as they'd strolled a moonlit beach, hand in hand. He'd been especially quiet and when she'd questioned, he'd blamed fatigue.

Something tickled at the edge of her memory, some featherlike itch of disquiet. Nothing Darrell had said but a feeling she'd experienced when they'd met another couple on the beach. A tight string of tension had vibrated in the balmy, ocean-scented air, though the conversation had been casual, an impromptu meeting of two couples on a Mexican beach.

In the aftermath of tragedy, Cassie had forgotten the encounter, but now she realized something had been off-kilter. The woman had complimented her brightly flowered skirt, a gift Darrell had purchased in the hotel souvenir shop. Nothing unusual about that. The odd thing had been the man's comment. What had he said?

Something about the price of roses had gone up.

The woman had laughed and said, "Oh, but you'll still buy them, won't he, Darrell? No matter the cost."

Darrell had said something in return, but his laugh had been dry and forced. And his hand against hers had been sweaty. She'd not thought much of it at the time. A brief moment on a beach with strangers.

Later, Cassie had asked about the couple and Darrell had

denied knowing them, saying they must have overheard her call him by name. She'd believed the easy explanation.

But now, in the light of what she knew, Cassie didn't think so. Darrell, she was convinced, had known the pair. The exchange about roses rang a strange, unsettling bell that echoed in her head. There was something. *Something.*

She gently placed Levi in his crib and hurried to her bedroom and the box containing photos and mementoes of a husband she had never really known. Darrell had lied to her, betrayed her, pretended to be someone he wasn't. It was time for her to stop protecting him. She'd come to accept that, as painful as it was. Somewhere in this box could be the answer.

She removed the items she'd copied for Heath and rifled through them, studying each one with a fresh eye. Photos, receipts, notes. Frustrated, she dumped the remaining items onto the bed. A colorful pair of maracas, whimsical, useless keepsakes like the jumping beans and a plastic drinking cup emblazoned with the hotel's logo. Souvenirs of a honeymoon that began in joy and ended in despair.

She gave the maracas a shake then put them aside to once more search through the bits and pieces of paper—the hotel bill, receipts.

She turned over a receipt, and there it was, though she'd looked at the page many times without seeing what was there. A small, handwritten notation on the delivery confirmation for a dozen roses, signed by Darrell. The air whooshed out of her lungs as she read, "The price of roses has gone up." And then a number to contact for more information.

She'd thought her new husband so wonderfully generous to order flowers for her every day. Now, she dug through the box for the other receipts, despising her suspicions. Hands shaking, she found another cryptic reference to roses and money and one with the words, "Delivery by Dias tomorrow night at 8. Room 2."

They hadn't stayed in room two.

Now she understood the note she'd found at the tornado site. Darrell had somehow used his gift of roses as a means to pass messages to drug contacts.

What a naive fool she'd been.

Heath was right. But like Darrell, Heath had used her for his purposes. She was doubly foolish and doubly humiliated.

At three rapid barks from outside, she shoved the receipts into her pocket. Though too early for Austin and Annalisa to return, she couldn't chance them seeing her tears. They'd never understand without the explanation she wasn't ready to give.

Tootsie shot off the bed, a furry cannonball, and ran for the door, yapping. Levi awakened, startled and began to cry. Dashing at her moist eyes, Cassie hurried to the nursery and picked him up.

"Shh. Shh," she murmured, gratified when his cries ceased the moment she snuggled him to her chest and went toward the barking dogs.

A shiny black SUV pulled into the drive. Her heart leapt, stuttered, hurt. Her legs felt like water.

"Heath." Quickly, she tamped back the glad reaction. He wasn't hers. He didn't love her. He was probably bringing her more bad news about the investigation.

Oh, Heath. You were right. And I don't want you to leave. But he would. She wasn't enough to keep him here.

Resolved to be strong, to give him the evidence and let him go without tears, Cassie stepped out on the porch and asked, "What are you doing here?"

Halfway to the porch, Heath froze in his tracks. Hers wasn't the greeting he'd hoped for. Yet there Cassie stood holding a baby and looking so motherly and beautiful, his whole being strained toward her. She was what he wanted—no, needed—in his life more than anything. This woman, a future together. The family they could make.

Holt was right. After God, a family and a woman to love kept a man grounded and filled. Heath had been running on empty for a long time.

On the drive from town he'd planned his speech, but now, with Cassie staring holes through him, the carefully arranged words abandoned him.

He started toward her, watched her mist-green eyes go from hurt resistance to bewilderment and then to resignation. Cradling the baby in the crook of her left arm, she reached into her pocket, withdrew a rumpled stack of paper and thrust it at him.

"You'll want to follow up on these, especially the phone number. I think Dias was Darrell's contact." Her voice was stiff and cool. She swallowed, revealing her stress. "Maybe his murderer."

She'd remembered something. He could see it in her eyes, the despair of knowing the truth. But he hadn't come about the case. At the moment, he didn't care about anything but her.

Almost rudely, he pushed her hand aside. "Later. I'm not here about the investigation."

"No?" She stepped back in surprise, wary as a doe. "Really? I thought that's all that mattered to you."

"The case can wait. This can't. I can't."

"Then why are you here? To say your goodbyes? Because I don't need that, Heath."

Her lips trembled and he despaired, knowing he caused her pain.

But a woman needed the words. Wasn't that what Holt advised?

"What if I'm the one who needs something?" He took a step toward her. She backed away.

"I can't help you anymore. Take the information and leave." She thrust the papers toward him again.

Really frustrated now, he stalked her until she backed into the wall of the house and further escape was impossible. "I need you, Cassie. You and only you. Forget the investigation, forget everything else."

Her mouth opened. Her lips trembled as her stoic expression began to melt like candle wax. She spun away. Her shoulders arched, heaved, and Heath berated himself. Was she crying?

"Cassie, don't. Please." He touched her shoulder. She stiffened but her body quaked.

From the corral, a horse whinnied, tail swishing at flies. Flashy pink flowers sprawled along the porch railing. Butterflies dipped and curtsied in the evening sun, supping the sweet-scented nectar. A man with his training missed none of the details, but he only had eyes for the woman.

He took her elbow and gently turned her to face him. "Cassie."

She shook her head and made a feeble attempt to pull away. "The baby."

"Can we go inside and talk? About us."

Her expression was stark and wounded, like a kicked puppy. "There is no us."

Heath's heart plummeted. Holt was wrong. Cassie wouldn't have him back. She wouldn't forgive him.

As if he felt the adult tension, the baby began to wail, a high-pitched, red-faced squall that split the air. Both of the big dogs winced and disappeared around the corner of the house.

Without a word, Cassie went inside the house and left

Heath standing alone. He felt like an idiot for coming, but better an idiot than never to know.

Jaw tight, he pounded on the door and then without permission, opened it and walked into the living room. He smelled pizza and would have smiled if the situation wasn't breaking his heart. His Cassie loved pizza. But she was nowhere in sight.

He raised his voice above the baby's cry. "I'm not leaving until you talk to me."

From down the hall, toward the nursery she'd proudly shown him, the baby quieted. A large sunburst clock above the fireplace ticked. The peach-colored poodle padded in to sniff his pants leg and then disappear into the nursery.

He'd already made a fool of himself. "Why stop now?" he murmured.

If Cassie wasn't going to come out, he'd go to her. With nothing more to lose but his pride, Heath strode to the open nursery.

"We're going to talk."

Cassie, leaned in to settle her nephew, turned her head. Her silky black hair swept across her cheeks. "Don't, Heath. This is hard enough without…"

"Without what? Without telling you that I made a terrible mistake? That I love you and if I could change what happened, the way it happened, I would? That I'd do anything to make things right?"

Slowly, she straightened, and Heath knew he finally had her attention.

"You do? You would?"

"I would. My entire adult life has been about my work and bringing honor to my dad. I was wrong about that, too. Life is so much more. Family and home and the right woman to love." When she didn't move, he said, "If you want me to grovel, I will."

"No." Then more emphatically, "No. Never."

But she didn't help him, either. "Then what will it take to win you back? What do you want? Name your price, Cassie, and it's yours."

She took a step toward him, reddened eyes swimming with emotion. "All I ever wanted was for you to love me. Truly love me."

"I do. I should have told you everything from the beginning, but I didn't know I'd love you this way. I've never felt like this about a woman before. Forgive me, Cassie. Let me be the man you need, the one you love."

"I don't know what's true anymore." She closed her eyes and put a hand to her forehead. A frown formed there, furrowing her brow. "I was wrong about Darrell and then about you. How do I know this time is right?"

He closed the gap until they stood a breath apart, not touching, but with everything in him, Heath longed to hold her and make up for all the hurt he'd caused. He longed to smooth away her frown with a kiss and make her smile again.

He tapped the place on his left chest. "Listen to your heart. You know. Hear my voice, see this man ready to go to his knees to gain your trust again." To prove his worth, he did exactly that. He went to his knees in front of her, took her hand and said, "I love you. After what you've been through, you'll say it's too soon and I promise not to rush you, but I know you're the one for me. I want to marry you, Cassie."

A gasp escaped her parted lips. "You do?"

"With all my heart. Say you love me, too, or tell me to hit the road. Your choice."

She stared at him for such a long moment that his stomach tumbled. In slow motion, she followed him down to her knees. The frown fled and wonder filled her expression.

"You're right." She touched the place over her heart. "I do know. In here." A beautiful smile lit her face. "I wish things had been different, but I can't hold a grudge. I love you, Heath. And I say yes."

A flood of joy and relief and thanksgiving rushed through him greater than any adrenaline thrill.

With a tenderness he didn't know possible, he cupped the face of his love and joined his lips to her soft, trembling ones. When she moved into his embrace and held him tight, he owned the world.

Epilogue

Two years later

On a Sunday afternoon in late spring, the skies filled with dark clouds and rain drenched the tulips as thunder echoed through the hillsides. The Blackberry River gushed over Whisper Falls and like a silver, curling ribbon circled past the town of the same name.

The people gathered in the fellowship hall of New Life Christian Church were accustomed to stormy springs and so they'd come anyway to share in the day's festivities.

Despite the damp outdoors, the interior of the hall was cozy, if humid, and thick with the scent of barbecued ribs from the newest restaurant in their growing town, Tony's Pig Stand. Haley's whimsical fairy vases centered each pink-clothed table with flowers from her garden. Annalisa and Lana had outdone themselves on the baby table. A pink and dark chocolate cake surrounded by chocolate-covered strawberries sat in the middle of tablecloth caught up with a bow. Above the table a printed banner proclaimed, "It's a girl!"

Children dashed through the building in a game of tag regardless of their mothers' efforts to calm them.

Voices chattered and laughter boomed in harmony with the thunder.

Cassie felt as if she was living in a dream as her friends and customers and family milled around the large hall in celebration of the child she'd never expected to have. They'd invited everyone they knew, and she was gratified for Heath's sake that the men had come, too.

"The guys will probably end up at the game tables in back," she said, smiling up at her husband of eighteen months.

"Not till they get their fill of these ribs." Heath pumped his eyebrows. "Gotta make up for not giving them a big wedding when we got married."

"True." They'd waited six months before exchanging vows. Heath claimed they were the longest six months of his life, but they'd gotten to know each other better and had time to fall deeper in love. When the day came, they'd promised "until death do us part" with a lifetime of conviction. The wedding had been small and spiritual with only family and closest friends in attendance, but this baby shower was huge!

"Do you think we ordered enough ribs and potato salad?"

"If we didn't, you can always call the Pizza Pan and order out thick pan pepperoni. You still have them on speed dial, don't you?"

Cassie grinned. "Don't torture me. I'm trying to eat healthy."

Heath placed a hand on her belly. At six months along, the baby wasn't yet huge but was more than the speed bump of a couple months ago.

"Proud of you." He kissed her on the cheek. He knew she'd become an unlikely champion of healthy eating and exercise and had even given up her highest heels for the sake of their unborn child. "Now, I'd better mingle with the guys or they'll call me a sissy."

She laughed and gave him a push. "Go. I want to talk babies with the girls anyway."

She went to the clutch of friends stacking baby gifts and keeping track of who brought what. Haley, Annalisa, Lana Davis and Louise directed the party, and all she had to do was enjoy.

"You'll have a ton of thank-you notes to send."

"Lucky me." And she meant that. Her life was blessed. Many friends and a wonderful family.

"Is that Heath's brother he's talking to?" Haley asked.

Cassie turned to look. "That one is Heston. Holt is with his mom, the dark-haired lady talking to my parents. They're with Miss Evelyn and Uncle Digger. See them over there?"

"Gorgeous men," Haley said.

Cassie bumped her shoulder. "You have a gorgeous man, too."

"Don't I know it? Look at how handsome he looks juggling the baby in one arm with Rose on his back."

"He's a good dad. How does Rose feel about having a brother?" Creed and Haley had a new baby boy, adopted two months ago.

"At four, she likes to play the big-sister role. But she might be a little jealous. We're working on that." Her auburn-haired friend gazed at her husband and children with such love, Cassie teared up. But then, everything made her tear up since she'd gotten pregnant.

She'd even cried when Lana had sung the national anthem at Pumpkin Fest last fall, her first clue that she was expecting a baby.

She sniffed and dabbed at her eyes with the balls of her hands. "I am the happiest woman in the world."

"Oh, honey." Lana gave her a quick hug. The tough girl had turned to a sugar cookie since her marriage to Davis Turner. She still wrote articles for the newspaper but her songwriting had found success in Nashville and she made frequent trips there for business. Cassie knew she grieved for the twin sister who'd never come home. They were still praying and believing that someday she would. "I'm happy for you."

"When are you and Davis going to have a baby?"

Since having Levi, now a toddler cowboy, Annalisa wanted all her friends to have a baby.

Lana blushed at Annalisa's question and reflexively touched her stomach. Four pairs of eyes followed the gesture.

"Are you pregnant, too?" Cassie asked.

"Shh. Don't say anything." Lana, unable to hide the grin, put a finger to her lips. "We're not ready to announce yet, and today is your day. But yes, I am."

The four women squealed and Cassie grabbed her friend in a hug, her belly bumping into Lana. "This only makes today more precious."

Lana fanned her flaming face with both hands. "I can't believe it. Sydney and Paige are twelve and Nathan's ten. Davis and I thought we might not have any more, but God had different ideas. I really, really wanted a baby, and Davis is over the moon." She laughed. "And a little shell-shocked."

"This is wonderful. I'll save all my baby things for you," Haley said. "Cassie can save hers, too. That way, whether you have a boy or a girl, you're covered."

"Speaking of baby things," Lana said, obviously to take the attention from her thrilling announcement. "Let's open presents!"

And so they did. Though they couldn't corral the gleeful children who were running on a sugar high from the cupcakes, the men and woman gathered around the mile-high gift table. The men, with good-natured machismo, rolled their eyes at the frilly, lacy clothes and needled their assistant police chief about the overdose of pink.

"The only thing keeping them inside is the storm," Cassie joked.

Standing behind her, Heath leaned down to whisper, "And the fact that I carry a gun."

Cassie giggled. From that wonderful day at the ranch, he'd never looked back. JoEtta had been thrilled at Heath's decision to remain on the force, and he'd become a terrific assistant police chief, a role he seemed to relish.

Cassie knew he'd rather be on the golf course today or at home watching baseball. The fact that he was at a baby shower, with her, made her love him more. This was, as he'd told her, his baby, too, and he didn't plan to miss a moment.

By the time the baby shower ended and people drifted away, amidst good wishes and promises of cookouts and dinners and haircuts, the storm outside had passed.

"You're tired, babe. We'll load the truck. You take it easy." Heath hoisted a new car seat while his brothers and their wives each gathered up boxes and bags.

Cassie paid him no mind. If her husband had his way, she'd stay in the recliner for nine months and knit. Her hunky man was a doting husband. "I'll bring the light stuff."

Arms loaded with diapers, she followed her husband out into the rain-washed evening. A glow gilded the cool, fresh atmosphere.

"There you go," Heath's brother Holt, whom she'd come to adore for his easy, teasing manner, slammed the truck's back door. "Everything is loaded."

"You guys go on," Cassie said. "I want to make one

more pass through the hall and make sure everything is restored to order."

Heath's mother took Cassie by the shoulders and kissed her cheek. "We'll meet you at the house. You look beautiful, dear."

Those pesky tears sprang to Cassie's eyes. She laughed to cover her embarrassment. "Thank you, Kate, for everything, especially for your son."

Kate gazed fondly at Heath who had circled around the car to chat with his brothers and Austin. "You're good for him, Cassie. He's happy now. Finally."

"He's made me happy, too. I can't begin to explain."

"You don't have to." Kate patted her arm. "See you at the house."

With a slam of car doors and engines, the last of the shower guests drove away, leaving Cassie and Heath alone. Cassie hugged herself, heart full, as her husband came toward her.

"I have something for you, but I wanted to give it to you when we're alone. With our families at the house, this may be our only moment today."

"Another present?"

"No, not exactly a gift, but closure." He tugged her hands free and held them, facing her. "Louis Carmichael was arrested last week in Arizona, trying to cross the border. Holt knew what this meant to us, Cassie, so he flew down there and spoke with Carmichael. Don't ask me how, but my brother has a way of getting people to talk."

"For which I will ever be thankful," Cassie said, knowing Holt was responsible for their reunion.

"Yes, well, Carmichael spilled some interesting beans. He blamed Darrell for ruining a good operation because of some woman."

"Me?"

"Apparently Darrell wanted out of the operation after he met you. Carmichael insisted he finish what he started or he'd tell you everything."

"And that last trip cost Darrell his life."

"Carmichael says he tried a double cross. Not smart and he paid for it. The man wasn't perfect, but he loved you, Cassie. You can stop kicking yourself for being fooled by him. He cared for you."

She laid her head on his shoulder and considered this latest revelation. Everything that had happened brought them to this moment. "He still used our honeymoon as a cover."

"Perhaps he did. But it's over now. You can be at peace with that part of your past."

"Yes." She'd long ago moved beyond the heartache and shame but Heath's news brought her peace and a much needed sense of closure. Carmichael was in jail and Darrell was not quite the villain she'd thought. She leaned back a little to meet her husband's gaze. "Thank you for telling me."

"My pleasure." He kissed her ear and sighed softly. "We've weathered some storms, haven't we, sweetheart?"

"Yes, we have. And we've come through stronger because of them."

She thought back to that stormy night when they'd met on a rain-slicked county road. To the tornado that ripped past town and opened up the can of worms left by Darrell and Louis. To the storm within from the hurt and heartache and confusion in the aftermath. Now, today, on the day of their baby shower another storm had rattled the windows and shook the skies. And as Heath said, they'd weathered them all.

"Look," he said, pointing over her shoulder.

Cassie spun in his arms, as much as a pregnant woman

can spin, to see a glorious rainbow arching above the little town of Whisper Falls.

"God's promise," she breathed, awed. "So beautiful."

"It reminds me of us." Heath slipped his arms around her from the back, his hands resting on their baby. "Life brings storms but there's always a rainbow. You're my rainbow, Cassie."

She leaned back against her man, resting in his strength and reveling in his love. Indeed, she thought as she looked at the glorious bow of color against the blue sky, they'd faced their share of storms, but the aftermath had been the most beautiful rainbow of all. A never-ending rainbow called love.

* * * * *

Dear Reader,

In *The Lawman's Honor,* Cassie and Heath bake brownies together, and the recipe mentioned is a favorite at our house. I thought you might enjoy it, too.

Brownies with Marshmallow Topping

1 box any brand brownie mix
¼ cup chocolate chips
½ cup chopped pecans or walnuts, optional

Mix brownies according to box instructions, add the chips and optional nuts. Bake as directed, taking care not to overcook. As soon as the brownies are removed from the oven, sprinkle with an additional ½ cup chocolate chips and enough mini marshmallows to sparsely cover the top. Cover the pan with a dish towel and let set for about five minutes. Then, while still warm and soft, use a spatula to marble the topping together, spreading well over the brownies. Can also sprinkle with additional nuts if desired. Instructions always say to cool before cutting, but they never last that long at my house. Enjoy!

I love hearing from readers. Contact me on Facebook, Twitter or through my website: *www.lindagoodnight.com.*
Until next time,

Linda Goodnight

Questions for Discussion

1. Who are the main characters in this story? Which was your favorite? Why? Can you describe him or her?

2. Cassie and Heath meet in an unusual way. What was it? Describe Heath's injuries and his reaction to them.

3. What was Heath's former job? Discuss his reasons for leaving. What is his new job?

4. Heath carries a special badge in his pocket. Explain its significance.

5. Discuss how Heath feels about justice and how those beliefs have affected his personal life.

6. A tornado strikes near the town of Whisper Falls. What is revealed by the storm that might otherwise never have been known? How does this affect each main character?

7. Cassie Blackwell is a well-liked businesswoman in Whisper Falls. What is her occupation? Who is her business partner?

8. Cassie has always lived at the ranch with her brother, but now worries she needs to move. Why? What has happened to make her feel like a fifth wheel?

9. Cassie is convinced she won't ever love again. Why? What happened to her first marriage?

10. Do you believe whirlwind relationships can ever work? Do you know someone who has met and married quickly? How did it work out?

11. Discuss the symbolism of storms in the story. How do the real storms relate to the characters' lives? Name a personal storm each one has faced.

12. Heath ascribes to the scripture, "the truth will set you free." To what or whom is the Bible referring in this text? Do you believe it applies to every situation, as Heath believes? Or is the Bible specific in context?

13. Heath begins the romance with Cassie for the wrong reasons. What were they? In your opinion, were his reasons justified? Why or why not?

14. Cassie doesn't want to believe the worst about her late husband. What is he accused of? How does this relate to her breakup with Heath?

15. Because of her loss, Cassie feels numb inside. In the beginning of the story, Cassie prays to feel again, but when her prayer is answered, she is unhappy. Have you ever prayed for something and then regretted it? Discuss.

16. Describe the book's resolution. How do Cassie and Heath work out their differences?

REQUEST YOUR FREE BOOKS!

2 FREE INSPIRATIONAL NOVELS
PLUS 2
FREE
MYSTERY GIFTS

Love Inspired

SPECIAL EXCERPT FROM

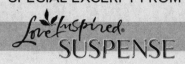
Love Inspired.
SUSPENSE

*Morgan Smith is hiding in the Witness Protection
Program. Has her past come back to haunt her?*

Read on for a preview of
TOP SECRET IDENTITY by Sharon Dunn,
the next exciting book in the
WITNESS PROTECTION series
from Love Inspired Suspense. Available April 2014.

A wave of terror washed over Morgan Smith when she heard the tapping at her window. Someone was outside the caretaker's cottage. Had the man who'd tried to kill her in Mexico found her in Iowa?

Though she'd been in witness protection for two months, her fear of being killed had never subsided. She'd left Des Moines for the countryside and a job at a stable because she had felt exposed in the city, vulnerable. She'd grown up on a ranch in Wyoming, and when she'd worked as an American missionary in Mexico, she'd always chosen to be in rural areas. Wide-open spaces seemed safer to her.

With her heart pounding, she rose to her feet and walked the short distance to the window, half expecting to see a face contorted with rage, or clawlike hands reaching for her neck. The memory of nearly being strangled made her shudder. She stepped closer to the window, seeing only blackness. Yet the sound of the tapping had been too distinct to dismiss as the wind rattling the glass.

A chill snaked down her spine.

Someone was outside.

If the man from Mexico had come to kill her, it seemed odd that he would give her a warning by tapping on the window.

She thought to call her new boss, who was in the guest-house less than a hundred yards away. Alex Reardon seemed like a nice man. She'd hated being evasive when he'd asked her where she had gotten her knowledge of horses. She'd been blessed to get the job without references. Her references, everything and everyone she knew, all of that had been stripped from her, even her name. She was no longer Magdalena Chavez. Her new name was Morgan Smith.

The knob on the locked door turned and rattled.

She'd been a fool to think the U.S. Marshals could keep her safe.

Pick up TOP SECRET IDENTITY wherever
Love Inspired® Suspense books and ebooks are sold.

Cowboy, wanderer… Father?

Nate Lyster and Mia Verbeek are in perfect agreement—that
letting someone new into your heart is much too risky.
Left on her own with four kids, Mia can't let just anyone
get close, while wandering cowboy Nate learned young that
love now means heartbreak later.

But when a fire turns Mia's life upside down, Nate is the only
one who can get through to her traumatized son—and her heart.
If Nate and Mia can forget the hurts of their pasts, they might get
everything they want. But if they let fear win, a perfect love could
pass them by….

A Father in the Making
by
Carolyn Aarsen

*Available April 2014 wherever
Love Inspired books and ebooks are sold.*

Find us on Facebook at
www.Facebook.com/LoveInspiredBooks

LI87878